W9-DDX-050

WHEN OLD MIDNIGHT COMES ALONG

AN AMOS WALKER NOVEL

WHEN OLD MIDNIGHT COMES ALONG

LOREN D. ESTLEMAN

THORNDIKE PRESS
A part of Gale, a Cengage Company

Fountaindale Public Library
Bolingbrook, IL
(630) 759-2102

GALE
A Cengage Company

Thorndike Press® Large Print Mystery.
The text of this Large Print edition is unabridged.
Other aspects of the book may vary from the original edition.
Set in 16 pt. Plantin.

LIBRARY OF CONGRESS CIP DATA ON FILE.
CATALOGUING IN PUBLICATION FOR THIS BOOK
IS AVAILABLE FROM THE LIBRARY OF CONGRESS

ISBN-13: 978-1-4328-7878-8 (hardcover alk. paper)

Published in 2020 by arrangement with Tor/Forge

Printed in Mexico
Print Number: 01   Print Year: 2020

In Memory of Sue Grafton
a giant of our trade
who never let her stature
interfere with the warmth of her person

I
Forgetting Paula

ONE

Lake St. Clair lay fallow at mid-morning, with no bright sail in sight. It was too early in the spring for the old Auto Money to expose its arthritis to the chill, and the New Rich were too busy trading in Japan before the stock exchange closed in Tokyo. The place was the Grosse Pointe Yacht Club, and I belonged there like a dead carp on Irish linen.

I was dressed as well as the budget would stand, cleaned, pressed, and polished; but the kind of trade the place encouraged could pass without challenge in sweats and sneakers. If you weren't born with that quality you had to practice six hours a day for years, like a bodybuilder. My work didn't take me into such circles often enough to justify the time.

"Walker? I'm Lawes."

I turned from the window and grasped the hand that was lent me. It was smooth but by no means soft, and gave the impression that the man who owned it was keeping some power in reserve. Francis Xavier Lawes wasn't as tall as he looked on television, but he was by no means short: a tightly packed five-nine and 160 in a charcoal suit, white-on-white cotton shirt, and sky-blue silk necktie, a combination so well coordinated it might have come all of a piece, to slough off at the end of the day and stand in a corner. He had sandy hair that would never go gray and plenty of it, a tan, clean-shaven face, and a youthful voice for a man of fifty.

"Mr. Lawes."

"You can call me X. Almost everyone does."

"Thanks. I'd like to test-drive it first."

The corners of his mouth stretched a centimeter, showing teeth that weren't too white or too even: Baby Bear teeth, likely by design. "They told me you were slow to commit."

"Who's they?"

"She, actually. Lieutenant Stonesmith. She inherited the investigation when Inspector Alderdyce retired."

"She recommended me?"

"Along with some others. I landed on you because you were the only one who special-

10

izes in finding missing persons."

"Looking for them, anyway."

"Have you had breakfast?"

I didn't say I didn't eat it under normal circumstances. Accepting a prospective client's offer to break bread is an important part of establishing a relationship; also I'd gotten in too late the night before to bother with supper. "No."

We strolled along the loggia, a cloisterlike passage open to the air that like the rest of the building was some dead architect's notion of life in Venice under the doge, passed through a couple of arches, and were shown by a headwaiter in livery to a white-cloaked table next to a window. There was a boat on the water now, square on the horizon, like a tin target being tugged along on pulleys in a shooting gallery. It was far enough across the water to have set sail from Canada.

At that hour we shared the room with a snowy-bearded gent in a blue blazer with a gold anchor on the handkerchief pocket and his dining companion, a black TV newsman I recognized from a local station. Blue Blazer was doing all the talking, gesturing with his fork, while his friend watched him without blinking.

"The Commodore's still looking to unload that World War Two minesweeper he's had since the Cuban Missile Crisis," Lawes said. "He started with the Fords; now he's worked his way down to the minor local celebrities. It's revealing how democratic the fatcats become when the bills pile up."

"I'm guessing you don't consider yourself a fatcat."

The muscles tugged again at his mouth. "Just a tabby who found his way to a sill in the sun."

Lawes paid tribute to the eggs Benedict. I said that would be fine. He checked two boxes on a menu card.

"Coffee, of course," he said. "And would you object to a mimosa?"

"That would be even better."

A server who looked like the maitre d's understudy collected the card. While we were waiting we watched the sail skimming across the top of the window. I asked Lawes if he kept a boat there.

"No, I'm what they call a Corinthian. Do you know what that is?"

"A Greek, isn't it?"

"At one time. Now it defines a man who enjoys sailing but doesn't own a boat. He has friends who do."

"That must simplify things."

"Well, you know what they say about the two happiest days in a fellow's life. My business affairs are complicated enough without cluttering up my private life with fees and maintenance."

"I know you're a public figure of some kind, but I'm not clear on what your business is."

"I liaise."

I gave him the same unblinking look the newsman gave the Commodore. He might have blushed a little; it's difficult to suppress it when you use words like *liaise* in regular conversation.

"When a contractor wants to do business with the city, it's my job to check him out and if he passes the test, to introduce him to the right bureaucrat."

"It seems to me someone went to jail for that not long ago."

"Well, that's how the position came to be. The reformers wanted someone legit who could count the horse's teeth, and if they add up, cut through the red tape without making a buck on the side. If the bidder turns out to be a phony or a chiseler or mobbed up, he never gets to see the inside of the municipal center. If I'm seen gobbling shrimp in the London Chop House with Vinny the Rhino Gotchabalzinmypocket, it's all in the line of duty. If it's anyone who buys time on Channel Two at election season, he retires from public service to spend more time with his family."

"What's it pay, if you don't mind my asking?"

"Enough to keep me from being tempted. Not enough to buy an island."

Our breakfast arrived. You could boil a lobster in the coffee and stand a spoon straight up in the cup. The eggs were good, for someone who is never hungry at that time of day. The champagne would be a premium label, but I couldn't tell it from hard cider. The orange juice they'd cut it with was fresh-squeezed and as perky as a puppy. I don't care for either any morning.

We ate and drank and told the Tigers how to take the pennant. Lawes was buying, so I let him direct the conversation. Finally he touched his napkin to his lips and said, "I need you to find my wife."

"I'll find her."

"You're that sure of yourself?"

"I never got a job being any other way."

"Is that a guarantee?"

I grinned. "No, sir. I'm not a plumber. But if I don't, no one else will. They'll just feed you vague leads and drain you till you decide to slip the hook."

"By God." He sat back. "By God, that's just what they've all done, starting with the gold standard boys with the fancy web sites and receptionists who talk like they fart tea and crumpets. I fell into the old trap, expecting Ferrari efficiency for Ferrari prices. I should've started at the end of the alphabet and worked my way back."

"You missed me, then. I list the place as A. Walker Investigations to appeal to short attention spans."

"I don't know how I *could* have missed you."

"You could. I only advertise in the Yellow Pages."

"Does that still exist?"

"On the beach. You can't impress girls by tearing a laptop in half." I pushed aside my plate. "Your wife can be found, assuming she didn't go someplace like Mars or Hollywood. If you don't get famous in the second place you might as well be in the first for all anyone ever hears of you. If she doesn't want to come back I can't fetch her."

"She won't give you any trouble there. She's dead."

Two

"Oh. You're *that* Lawes."

He nodded. "I thought you'd make the connection sooner or later. The details remain more vivid than the names."

"What's it been, five years?"

"Six last month."

Lawes's wife, a professional woman, had missed an appointment northwest of Detroit. Her car was found abandoned an hour or so later in a seedy neighborhood clear on the other side of the city. She hadn't been seen since and an intense police investigation had turned up nothing. Unexplained disappearances, particularly involving people of some prominence, was red meat for reporters weary of covering routine murders. The story blazed for a week, then sputtered out, to flare up on slow days and in Sunday supplements whenever an anniversary of the event came up.

"I withdraw my pitch," I said. "Six years

or six hundred amount to the same thing. A cadaver-sniffing dog couldn't dig her up now."

A nerve in his left cheek jumped. "Stonesmith said you were blunt. She might have added *brutally.*"

"I'm sorry."

"Don't be; that I can still react after all this time might surprise some of the people I meet in the course of my profession. Anyway, sympathetic platitudes waste time. I'm resolved to the loss, and I'm ready to move on. That requires evidence that Paula's deceased."

"Why not just wait another year? I'm shaky on precedent, but I seem to recall that seven years with no proof to the contrary is standard for a legal declaration of death."

"It's not that clear-cut; but then neither is the exception. If you can prove in court that a missing person is dead, the seven-year rule is waived. *After* seven years, if you want to have a missing person declared alive, you must prove the party is not dead."

"Congratulations."

"What's that mean?" His voice had bark on it.

"Aristotle." I rolled a shoulder. "Another Greek. He said you can't prove something isn't; only that it is."

17

"I can't do either. That's why I invited you here."

"So wait it out."

He shook his head. "This pitch is going the exact opposite of what I'm used to. You're supposed to convince me you're the one for the job, and I'm supposed to be the one who's reluctant."

"Believe me, it's not a habit I want to get into. I'm not against getting my hands dirty, but when I do I like to know the reason. What's another eleven months after all this time?"

"I want to remarry. Does that satisfy you, or are you still so young you need me to spell it out?"

"I'm older than you are. Who's the impatient one, you or the lady?"

"That's our concern."

"Okay."

A pair of eyes narrowed. "Then why did you ask?"

I drained my flute. The champagne had gone flat. "I'm curious by nature, Mr. Lawes. It's a requirement on the application form for spooks, spies, and private eyes."

Our waiter made the usual polite inquiries, then handed Lawes a piece of paper, which he signed slashingly. The man cleared the table and excused himself from my life.

"So are you hired?"

I told Lawes what I needed, beginning with a check. When it snuggled up against my chest, he drew an oyster-colored phone from an inside pocket and scrolled until he found several shots of Paula Lawes taken within the past ten years. She was a tall slim redhead with an angular jaw who if she were alive would still be several years younger than her husband. The first thing I decided about her was she didn't enjoy smiling for cameras. "I'll send these to your cell," he said. "What's the number?"

I gave it to him. "It's only good for calls. You'd better print them out. I'll drop by your office later."

A gold watch got consulted. "I have appointments. I won't be in before two."

"That's fine. I need to brush up on the official record first: Shine the seat of my pants before I start burning shoe leather."

We stood and I shook the strong dry hand again.

WDIV, the call letters for Channel 4, worked out of a limestone pile on West Lafayette, between the old Detroit *News* and *Free Press* buildings; which back when newspapers mattered must have made for some lively conversation in the Anchor Bar where the employees of all three institutions hung out. Rusty Donovan met me on the soundstage, skipping over and around coils of thick cable on the polished concrete floor. Lights blazed near the far wall, where a meteorologist in a sharp suit rehearsed his pantomime in front of a blue screen.

"Been a spell," he said when he had his hand back. "I thought by now you'd joined the mass migration to Florida."

Everything about Rusty looked washed out except his eyes, which were the intense blue of marbles: His hair, lashes, and what skin showed between his freckles were a kind of faded pink, with a sickly green cast from the light coming through his eyeshade. His flannel sleeves were rolled up tight past muscular forearms with a U.S. Marines eagle tattooed on the right.

I grinned. "The gas alone would use up my retirement stake. You free?"

"I'm the shop steward for Local two-nine-nine. What do you think?"

"I think they'll fire you when we go to war with Nebraska."

"If then. Let's see what's on the tube."

I'd called to tell him what I needed. He got another technician's attention and jerked his thumb toward the talent practicing his gestures in front of the screen. The tech nodded, grabbed a pole on wheels with a bank of lights on top, and rolled it that direction. I followed Rusty out of the room, down a hallway lined with unpainted dry-wall, and through a door into a cramped space made even tighter by a control panel and rows of monitors. On all of them something was going on: a police dashboard cam chasing an erratic SUV on what looked like I-696; a real-time tower shot of down-town; a female reporter in a car coat and beret reading from a notepad in front of the Frank Murphy Hall of Justice; three sheet-covered bodies being wheeled on gurneys out of a house on Any Street, Detroit; the meteorologist on the soundstage making wide swooping movements in front of what was now a map of Southeastern Michigan.

Rusty pointed his chin at a male reporter standing just clear of a gushing broken water main. "There's Roddy, picking his nose again. Next time let's go live."

"Sure," said the man seated at the panel. "*Me* they'll can."

"I'll get you back in a week, Sid, with a raise. Cue it up."

Sid was black, with a bald dome that gleamed like an eggplant in a mist of gray hair scraped close to the temples. He flipped a switch and the weatherman disappeared.

Another switch and something fluttered on the monitor, then assumed shape, first as a still shot, then a picture in motion. A time- and date-stamp in the lower left corner belonged to another year. I looked at a different female reporter holding a microphone for a thick-built white-haired cop in uniform with a cap bearing the scrambled eggs of a precinct commander. Other men and women, some in uniform also, passed back and forth between where they stood and a low-slung sedan parked on a paved street near the top of a hill. It was night, but arc lights turned the scene bright as noon.

The questions and answers were strictly boilerplate: An unnamed witness, what the first responders found at the scene, unspecified leads, pleas for anyone with information to come forward.

Paula Lawes, the wife of prominent local businessman Francis X. and a consultant with the Detroit-based public relations firm of Baylor, Schneider, Baylor, and Baylor, had missed an appointment with a client in Farmington Hills, one of the city's more prosperous suburbs, and had not been seen since leaving the office. Her car had been discovered in much-less prosperous Allen Park, clear on the other side of the city from where she'd been expected, with the driver's door wide open and her purse open on the front seat. Among the usual stuff inside were her credit cards, a couple of hundred in cash, and her cell phone. That shot all to hell the theory that her car was stolen on the way to the meeting and driven there by the thief, if plain robbery was the motive.

Presumably an editor or someone had spliced footage of the entire investigation onto one reel (or whatever unit of technology had replaced film and videotape since the century turned) for a retrospective, because the scene shifted to reporters camped out in front of the Lawes house in Birmingham waiting for the husband to appear and be interviewed, then to a press conference during which the Detroit Chief of Police announced that he'd assigned the city Homicide detail to assist Allen Park in the investigation, then a talking-head panel of criminalists, psychiatrists, and palmists offering their opinions. When Lawes came on finally, hastening with his lawyer from the old Third Precinct, for several years the home of Homicide, through a crowd of journalists after he'd been cleared as a suspect, I asked Sid to switch off.

No blood, no unexplained DNA, none of the obligatory signs of struggle; just the sudden and complete nonexistence of a fellow carbon-based creature, with nothing to fill the space she'd left for days, then weeks, then months, then more annihilation yet when the media shifted their attention to other events.

We stared at the blank screen for a moment. Then the bald technician worked a switch and the meteorologist sprang back into view, pushing a big yellow H across Lake Huron with both hands.

Rusty said, "Man, that's one ice-cold potato. They must be paying you by the hour."

I thanked Sid and slapped Local 299 on the back. "Miami Beach, here I come."

THREE

The old gray lady at 1300 was still standing, with no sign out front announcing it was under new management. Every time I go there I expect it to have been sold to China along with the rest of downtown.

Most of the Detroit Police Department had bugged out of the Romanesque building on Beaubien to escape dry rot, vermin, roof leaks, and carcinogenic building materials, taking up temporary residence in various precinct houses around the city. "Temporary" is one of the more worked-out adjectives in our town: Everything's waiting, from condemned HUD houses to jungle-growth empty lots to a multimillion-dollar graft job of a jail, decaying in an unfinished state. The city itself bumps along under the provisional oversight of the state treasurer and the FBI, with no say from its couple of dozen voting citizens; elections here draw as much attention as washday.

Deborah Stonesmith was a steel post amid all this cardboard. She'd been on the force fourteen years, working her way up from Stationary Traffic to the Criminal Investigation Division (Major Crimes Unit) with the rank of detective lieutenant. She'd staked out permanent territory in an office partitioned off from the rest of the third floor at venerable 1300, mostly to make use of the lateral space left behind by most of the department: Give her a table, a ream of paper, and a month of uninterrupted concentration and she'd find the princes in the Tower.

In the ground-floor lobby a desk sergeant sat frowning at a clipboard across from a dusty gift shop, where you can browse a display of baseball caps, coffee mugs, shot glasses, and swizzle sticks all bearing the DPD logo while you're waiting to post bail for a loved one. The metal detector shuddered a little when I passed through it, but that was just the pins from an old rib injury, so no one tackled me. Two medium-size patrolmen joined me in the elevator, inserting themselves sideways. On the third floor I pried myself loose with a shoe horn and stumbled out.

I was in the stomping ground of the old Racket Squad, where if you closed your eyes

26

and subtracted mildew and rat urine, you could still smell cigars, rye whiskey, and *eau de* rubber hose.

The usual tarry coffee made gargling noises in an urn on a metal table under a corkboard shingled with wanted circulars going back to Dr. Richard Kimble. She was there, dandling a tea bag in a stoneware mug labeled WORLD'S GREATEST AUNT.

"Garage sale find?" I said by way of greeting.

A pair of eyes like brown asteroids registered no surprise at my presence. "My sister's kid," she said. "I raised her after her mother went into rehab the third time. Kept her clean, gave up all my weekends to soccer, which is only a little more exciting than watching dead goldfish float, put her through vocational school, paid her rent for a year, and all I got was this crummy mug." But she smiled as she sipped from it.

She was tall for a woman and some men, but it was all distributed so that you didn't notice it until she was standing in front of you, with prominent facial bones and dark reddish-brown hair worn lately in a shoulder bob. Her suit, coral trimmed with gray, was cut loosely, but followed her contours closely enough that you wouldn't mistake her for a man from any angle. Not a beautiful woman or even pretty, but striking; a black Katharine Hepburn.

"I need a favor," I said. "At this point I can't remember who owes who."

"Horseshit. I know all about your little blue notebook. You can trace every marker back to Coleman A. Young."

"They don't go back that far, mostly because Hizzoner had a little blue book of his own, only his had dollar signs. How'd you find out about mine, drones?"

"On this city's budget? We farm out all our black ops to jail trusties. Don't try to bluff the house, Walker. You're so deep in the red you look like Jack the Ripper."

"So get out *your* little blue book and compound the interest."

"Uh-uh. I'm not as easy as Mary Ann Thaler. Hear from her lately?"

"You ever hear from a cop you helped put in stir?"

"Christmas card, every year. Posed with his sweetie last time. Sweetie had him a tattoo of Evander Holyfield on his right cheek."

"*Which* right cheek?"

"There's a lady present." She took another sip, pulled a face, gave the bag a couple more ducks. "What wringer are they in, and who belongs to 'em?"

28

"Matrimonial bliss, and Francis X. Lawes."

"He calls it bliss? What'd he do, go out and get himself born again?"

"Next thing to. He says he wants to remarry, but there's this obstacle that he's still hitched unless and until a man with a rubber stamp says his wife's dead."

"Tell him to wait. The statute must be coming up, and then it's just a matter of a sit-down with a judge."

"Just over a year to go. Apparently it's too long."

"For whom, the groom or the bride?"

"He didn't say, so of course it's the bride. Anyway I'd like to see the file. Me and the Eyewitness News team got different ideas of what's fit for the folks at home."

"No objections, so long as it doesn't leave this building. We won't be tripping over each other. I've got obsessions of my own without taking on hand-me-downs."

Our paperless society has killed more trees than an army of Paul Bunyans; nobody, Silicon Valley included, trusts memory banks. Cops especially never throw anything away. If you have the time to waste you can browse the *L*s in storage at 1300 and bone up on every case from the Lindbergh kidnapping back to Lot's wife. Evidently they all had a local connection.

A civilian employee of the department, a retired officer from the look of him, whose face had frozen into a grimace around the time of the '67 riots, rode up from the basement and pushed a stiff cardboard storage carton on a mail cart into an unused office on the floor above Stonesmith's. A row of departed file cabinets had left square footprints in the asbestos tile and a *Girls of Baywatch* calendar hung at an expressionistic angle from a nail on a wall: In that room, time had stopped at March 1993.

When the cart trundled off on a rickety wheel I was left alone with a gray steel desk, a swivel that listed to starboard, and stacks of green cardboard folders, each bound with a rubber band, the first of which crumbled when I touched it, without any effect on the bundle of onionskin reports, grainy photographs printed on cheap stock, old skin cells, coffee rings, and stale nicotine.

That last made me want to commit a misdemeanor. I found the smoke detector, a grubby white plastic Frisbee mounted in a corner of the suspended ceiling, and got up on tiptoe to dismantle it. I could have saved myself the trouble; the four AAA batteries inside were leprous bulges of corrosion. I sat down, got a Winston going, and used an open drawer for an ashtray. I wasn't the first; when I drew it out, a flock of gray flakes fled across the bottom like silverfish.

As page-turners went it wasn't Tom Clancy, or even *Thomas the Tank Engine.* I spotted some trademark phrases a certain breed of prowl-car cop uses to stay awake to the end of the shift, a couple of inside jokes, the usual creative misspellings, and a lot of patrician vocabulary — almost invariably cocked up — intended to land a cushy job as a department spokesman, but mostly the reports were a lesson on how to make a possible murder investigation read like a pitch for pet health insurance.

The transcripts of interviews told a different story. Frances Xavier Lawes had been subjected to more intense scrutiny than had been reported by the press. Most people assume the wealthy can buy anything they want, without questioning the cost. Like most wealthy people, the Laweses were broke; not the way you and I and the majority of the race are broke — they can always swing seven figures in credit, if they cared to stand for the legal loansharking — but manicured hands wring as frequently as the working man's. The couple was overextended at home and in vacation houses in

Arizona and Florida, barely making payments on a small fleet of automobiles, and no closer to getting out from under their credit cards than they were at the start. Husband and wife had their lives insured for a million apiece; and then there was the old adage that when a spouse vanishes or dies under a cloud of suspicion, most investigations needn't look beyond the surviving partner. All told, Lawes had spent more time at headquarters than most of the lightbulbs, and search warrants were executed on his office and all three of his residences; but as the days, weeks, and months wore on and no body was recovered, common sense kicked in: Before considering to lift a finger to discuss cutting a check, insurance companies insist on proof of death. If money was the motive, Lawes would have arranged a discovery somehow. That's how cops think, in a line as straight as the ones they draw for suspected drunk drivers, and it pays off usually. Lawes got a clean bill of health — without prejudice in case the smoke drifted back his way — and so far as the record was concerned, that was still the situation six years later.

I got a whiff of something, though; call it gut instinct or jaded expectations or the Police Pox — extremely contagious if you spent too much time in their proximity — but if, say, the Michigan Department of Transportation plowed up a pile of bones digging a new exit ramp for I-696 and they bore a scrap of Paula Lawes's DNA, Frances X. would open his door to a Homicide detective with a new warrant in his paw inside twenty-four hours; not counting Sunday when the courthouse is closed.

Someone's foot bent a board outside the room and kicked a piece of 1300 across linoleum. I extinguished a cigarette, more from respect for the someone's intelligence than guilt, and blew smoke out through the gap in the window frame. Deb Stonesmith opened the door without knocking, sniffed the air, shrugged. "You had an hour and a half; should be plenty. Want me to gather the suspects, ask Archie to bring a fresh orchid down from the plant room?"

"I'm not Nero Wolfe," I said. "I'm not even near enough. Is this everything? Blu-ray was new when the last report was filed."

"Perps don't stop perpetrating while we chew over old cases. You know what we know, unless you skipped the boring parts."

"There should be a record of the last time Lawes pressed for news."

"There is. You read it."

I shuffled papers, found it. "He hasn't

asked for an update in four years?"

"Touching, ain't it? Just pining away."

"Is that why someone decided he killed her?"

She played with the latest tea bag. "Did someone decide that? Maybe I should brush up on the file."

"Not everything makes it into writing. Who's got a hard-on against my client and why?"

"I can answer the first question. He'll have to answer the second. John Alderdyce."

"The inspector's retired, I heard."

"From the department. I never heard of any detective giving up detecting. He's with the Reliance agency now." The smile she built bore no resemblance to the one she'd kept for her niece. "Stay on your toes, Amos. The competition just got stiffer."

FOUR

The late Ernest Krell was the offspring of a bat and one of those fish that live so many fathoms from sunlight they're born without eyes. Sometime in the seventies he bought a vacant warehouse on the river for pennies, converted the vast hollow interior into offices, and covered the brick exterior with polished aluminum, eliminating all the windows. The excuse was that as a security consultant he preferred his walls solid and unbreachable, but my personal opinion is he was as crazy as wax fruit. For years the place looked like a bouillon cube wrapped in foil.

That had changed with the founder's death. His grandchildren had come to town long enough to hear the will and appoint someone to manage the business, then caught the return flight to Seattle. The contractor the manager hired carved slits from the roof to the foundation, installed tinted Plexiglas in the spaces, and covered the rest with ruddy stucco. Copper letters in relief spelled out RELIANCE SECURITY SERVICES across the front of the building. A row of squat concrete posts discouraged car bombers from rushing the entrance.

I'd spent much of my career giving Reliance no discernible competition, and part of it running errands for it; the kind Krell didn't consider worth creasing his pumps over. Since his passing, the firm had concerned itself more with anti-terrorism and less with pesky fleabites such as missing persons and embezzlers; my meat.

A map of the continental U.S. decorated the floor tiles in the vaulted lobby, studded with brass stars to mark the cities where the company had branches; you could hop-scotch from Detroit to Denver on them without straining your groin. An oiled-bronze bust of Krell scowled on a pedestal atop Topeka. The sculpture was the size of the tub they scald hogs in. A brass plate riveted to the base read:

JULIUS ERNEST KRELL
(1928–2011)

Beneath this were engraved likenesses of the Distinguished Service Cross, the Purple

Heart, and the Oak Leaf Cluster. Krell had completed two tours in Korea and retired from the United States Secret Service after fifteen years. Steel-framed photos of the great man chatting up various commanders-in-chief encircled the walls; not that he'd ever served on any of the presidents' details. He was photo-bombing long before anyone thought to give it a name.

A middle-aged woman in a blue serge suit with a necktie-and-handkerchief set occupied a cockpit in front of the elevators. I told her I was there to see John Alderdyce. I handed her a card.

"Appointment?"

I shrugged, looking sheepish. She lifted the handset from a piano-like console and pressed a key. When someone answered she read my card into the mouthpiece, listened, hung up. "Four-ten."

A corridor painted buff and blue — FBI colors — encircled the top floor. More 3-D copper characters identified otherwise blank doors. I passed a series of vertical slits facing the river, glancing in at a couple of open doors where men in vests sat drinking coffee and diddling keyboards. The vests were a holdover from the previous management. It was worse when the old man was in charge: Jackets were required at all times as a condition of employment. I rapped at 410, which was closed.

"Okay, Walker."

I'd known John Alderdyce since we sneaked smokes behind Munger Junior High, and I can count on my elbows how many times he'd addressed me by my first name. I opened the door and found him stretched out in shirtsleeves and stocking feet on a pale blue Naugahyde couch, scribbling on a sheet of paper using a folded copy of the *Free Press* for backing. A metal desk, pale blue also, stood in front of glass shelves lined with family photos in stand-up frames, a baseball on a wood pedestal signed by the 1968 Tigers, and that official-office staple, the Michigan Penal Code, interred in red-cloth coffins for all eternity.

Apart from a pair of black-rimmed reading glasses, he hadn't changed much since he'd made detective lieutenant with the Detroit Police Department, before we went to war for some reason in Grenada. A few extra pounds rode comfortably enough on his six-foot-two, rawboned frame, and retirement from the civil service hadn't changed his taste in tailoring; from salmon-colored linen shirt to gray lisle socks, he wouldn't be sniffed at by the editors at *GQ*. Black men, whites too, tend to get paler with age, but his face still looked as if it had been carved from a solid block of anthracite. Steel shards glittered in his close-cropped hair.

When he turned the sheet over I got a glimpse of what he'd been working on: a fair amateur rendition of Tweety Bird in a cage.

"Don't they usually put the break room on the ground floor?"

He started doodling on the blank side. "This is as busy as it gets. When the old snoop died, he took the company's gravitas with him. I came at the end of a long line of former state attorney generals, G-men, and specialists in animal control, all of whom turned down the job. 'John J. Alderdyce, Detroit Police Inspector, Retired, Consultant' looks good on the letterhead, with the occasional appearance behind a podium for the benefit of the ladies and gentlemen of the press when the firm cracks a case they give a shit about. They pay me more than the Chief of Police to lie here and whack off with a company pen."

"What's the *J* stand for?"

"I'm thinking Jupiter; it's got the ring of smiting to it, don't you think? I don't have a middle name, but the straw boss of the moment says that just looks common in embossed lettering."

"I don't see it lasting. I'm not talking about the middle initial."

"I figure I'll stick till I run out of stationery. Then I'll go down to H.R. and date the letter of resignation they've got on file." He folded the sheet into an airplane and sent it sailing into a corner. He scowled. "Don't look at me in that tone of voice. Our grandson moved in with us: 'Just till I pay off my student loan, Pop-pop.' Care to know what four years at Michigan cost?"

"Seriously, 'Pop-pop'?"

He snapped his glasses shut, slid them into his shirt pocket, swung his feet to the floor and into glossy cordovan slip-ons. "What do you want, Walker?"

"Paula Lawes."

"Christ. Why not start with who blew up the *Hindenburg* and work your way forward?"

"Her husband says he wants to get married again, and society frowns on a man taking a new wife when the old one's unaccounted for. He wants me to account for her."

"I bet he does. There's a little matter of a million in life insurance benefits waiting in escrow until you do."

"Is that why you didn't want to let go of him?"

"Talk to Lieutenant Stonesmith. It's her beef now."

"I did. She lent me the file. If you'd had Lawes under your roof a couple more days, you could claim him as a dependent."

"I play the percentages. You know the stats when there's a spouse in the picture, and how far they go up when there's money involved."

"It wasn't my first time studying an investigation you headed up. You've filled a couple of cellblocks with cons you broke with less than half the effort you put into Lawes. Fifty fresh homicides crossed your desk while you were working him, all just as juicy and some of them with a closer sell-by date. What made him your white whale?"

"If it wasn't your first time in the files, you'd see what was missing as well as what was there."

Apart from the padded swivel that went with the desk, the only other seat was a goosed-up director's chair made of chromium and blue leather. I used it, crossed my legs, and laced my fingers across my right knee. "So he wasn't in your hip pocket pushing for results. A lot of married couples who aren't very close don't kill each other.

41

Probably the majority; but then I'm a fan of human nature and could be wrong."

"You're wrong. Not about the majority of innocents, but about being a fan of the race. Your glass has been half empty as long as I've known you."

"Not always. It depends on what's in the glass. And I'm still waiting for an answer."

He got up and unhooked his suitcoat from the back of the swivel; shrugged into it and sat down. Same old Alderdyce, in uniform now and on the job. "You committed? Not just testing the bathwater with your elbow?"

"I haven't cashed his check yet, but yeah."

"Make sure it clears. You know how rich people are about paying their bills."

"I get it. You don't like him."

"I bet my pension on him the first time we spoke and all the times after that. It's not evidence, just something you hear out the corner of your ear: Something someone says, or how he says it, lands with a thud instead of a clang. You notice it right off, but you can't pin down just what it is at first. Then every time you hear it later you're surer than ever he's your man. I guess even a plastic badge experiences that from time to time."

I nodded, tossing the plastic-badge crack over my shoulder like spilled salt. It was just habit on his part.

"You've dealt with the newly bereaved," he said. "Even when it's obvious someone's dead, they usually use present tense first, then catch themselves as it sinks in."

"Not always, but often. Go on."

"I'd argue in favor of always when it's a missing person, especially when it's as recent as a couple of hours, when there's still plenty of reason to hope. Not Francis X. Lawes. From the start, he referred to his freshly absent wife in the past tense. Not once, then or later, did he ever say, 'Paula is.' It was 'Paula was,' right from the time the Allen Park police knocked on his door with the troubling news. Who does that?"

"Let me guess. Rich people?"

"Murderers, that's who. And not just passion killers driven to violence in the heat of the moment. He'd been thinking of her as dead for some time, even when she was still alive and present. And for him she was. Face it, Walker. You're representing O.J., without the entourage."

FIVE

"What kept you from pinching him?"

"Couldn't break his alibi. He was attending a governors' conference on Mackinac Island; witnesses and photos up the wazoo. That doesn't mean he couldn't have hired it, but none of our leads in that arena panned out."

"That's it, then? Just your gut?"

He spread his hands, each of which could palm a medicine ball. "If I had anything better, he'd be in stir; in isolation, where they put the VIP killers so they don't have to mingle with the riffraff. If you think there's no class system in this country, drop in on any joint on visiting day and count the contusions and lacerations on the poor schnooks that picked pockets and stole bicycles."

"Any objection if I run it out?"

"Why ask? I'm strictly private sector, like you."

"Not like me."

"I've still got friends in harness, but they won't be pulling you over for a broken tail-light that wasn't broken when they pulled you over. I won't squawk if somebody else gets this collar. It's never been about the credit.

"This is the job every P.I. waits his entire career to land: Give the client what he's paying for — Paula Lawes's bones, or proof that bones is all she is — and it'll reopen the investigation. If it's a body, the lab rats will establish cause of death, and the CID will turn over the dominoes from there, all the way back to who provided the cause. If it's a witness, that's even better; the working detectives can eliminate the white coats, roll up their sleeves, and get cracking. If by some fluke it doesn't lead to the grieving widower, it's still justice; if it does — and it will — it's satisfaction all around. When the file's closed this time, they'll put your name on your own personal coffee mug at Thirteen-hundred. In this town that's Olympic gold. I shouldn't have to tell you that."

When he shook his head, it was like the Great Barrier Reef swaying in the sea breeze. "For someone smart enough to get rich, Lawes can't see past the wedding night. He could've let things stay as they were for a year and cruise off into the sunset with his new squeeze, but instead he's let his dick lead him square into harm's way. His dick and a million he can't get without proof of death.

"My friends are yours, Walker. Anytime, night and day, weekends and holidays included. It beats Walmart."

When I eat breakfast I'm rarely hungry before supper, but I had time to kill before collecting those pictures of Paula Lawes. I had pie and coffee uptown and tamped down my indigestion over some reading in the public library.

Shortly after the feds locked up our most recent bent mayor, one of the swanky monthlies that tried to make Detroit look glamorous had run a puff piece about sweeping changes in the way the city was managed. Near the bottom of the third column on the second page was a photo of Francis X. Lawes shaking hands with the appointed chief of the new administration. I folded the magazine back and showed the picture to the vagrant eating a raw onion hoagie at the next carrel over. "This guy look like a killer to you?"

His red eyes clashed with the lavender

rings around them. He stared at the picture, belched blue fire, and bit into his sandwich with a crunch that shook the building.

"Yeah, me too," I said.

If you want to know how the local sports teams are doing, but aren't curious enough to read a paper or watch TV, swing by the Coleman A. Young Municipal Center. There, in front of the blank wall facing Woodward Avenue, squats *The Spirit of Detroit,* a ton or so of verdigris copper, popularly known as the Jolly Green Giant, holding a radiating sphere aloft in one hand and a nuclear family in the other. If at playoff time it's wearing a huge jersey carrying the insignia of the Tigers, Lions, Red Wings, or Pistons, we've got a dog in the hunt. This year it just had its breechclout, and it was lucky to still have that.

Francis X. Lawes dealt city services to private contractors from a small suite on the fifteenth floor, far enough away from the current mayor's office on Nineteen to quash suspicions of too much elbow-rubbing. According to the article I'd read, the company rented the space from the city and the CEO collected no commissions on the construction and maintenance contracts he negotiated; he worked entirely on salary, out of which he paid his staff. Just how much that was didn't make the piece.

A long walk down a windowless hall brought me to a plain door with a plastic card in a slot, containing only the suite number and THE LAWES GROUP in white letters. It looked like the entry to the office of a community-college instructor who doubled as the coach of the debate team.

The reception room wasn't much larger than mine, and although the furniture was newer (my budget managed old, avoiding the suspicious aura of antiquity) and the walls cheerier — tangerine, eggshell blue, moss green, and cream yellow alternating — whoever decorated it probably wouldn't have set me back more than a year's income.

It was all very modest and understated, including the young woman behind the desk with her strawberry blond hair caught behind her head and eyeglass frames to match, a far cry from the gangsta plush of a couple of previous administrations, and wouldn't have raised an eyebrow in a room full of federal watchdogs. Community-service certificates in frames were the sole decoration. It was unpretention bordering on pretentious; one more sign of responsible spending and I'd have pegged it as stage art. After a certain point, a penny saved is a dollar skimmed.

I told her who I was and that her boss was expecting me. She used an intercom and asked me to take a seat.

"Thanks. I've done enough of that today. They say sitting is the new smoking."

She was turning that over to look at the other side when one of three communicating doors opened and a woman who was not as tall and not as bony and not at all as black as Deborah Stonesmith came in, although she was tall and slim enough. Her hair was short, cut in bangs at a thirty-degree angle on a broad forehead, and way too pale for someone in her mid-thirties; white is the new blond. It contrasted sharply with her Florida tan. Eyes brown with gold flecks, mile-high cheekbones, a chin that imitated the contours of a pear-shaped diamond. Her neck wasn't quite long enough to tie in a knot. White heavy-silk blouse, French cuffs linked with onyx, snug gray skirt cut like her bangs, starting two inches above her right knee angling down to two inches below her left. Oxblood patent-leather pumps on her feet, with four-inch heels. The angle, combined with the altitude, made me feel a little queasy, but that might have been the imported pie and smelted-lead coffee I'd had for lunch. She stood with arms folded loosely and one trim ankle crossed in front of the other, a runway pose.

"Perhaps I can help? I'm Holly Pride. I manage the office."

"It's nice to meet you, but I didn't order a Holly Pride. I'm waiting on a Francis X. Lawes."

"Mr. Lawes is busy at the moment, Mr. — ?" She raised arched eyebrows at the blonde, who mouthed my surname. "— Walker. I'm in charge of all the business conducted by The Lawes Group."

"I'm not here on Lawes Group business. My business is with Lawes."

I got the full body scan. I didn't have to wait three days for the result: wrong suit, wrong shoes, wrong face. "Will you follow me, please?" She reversed her ankles, turning her body in the direction of the door she'd come through.

"As long as it leads to Lawes."

"We'll see."

I'd run all my lines, and in any case the blonde behind the desk was showing too much interest in the matinee. Holly Pride held the door for me and I entered an office with a window offering a view of the Detroit River. It seemed I couldn't get away from the river today. It was a fairly Spartan setup,

50

in keeping with the rest of the place: pastel blue walls, architect's steelpoint drawings in plain frames, a flat-panel desk holding up the usual equipment, including a stand-up photo with its blank back facing me.

She leaned her hips back against the desk and crossed her ankles the other way. When she did the same with her arms, a ring on her left hand sent off strobes. I shifted positions to keep the glare out of my eyes.

"Holly Pride," I said.

"Right the first time." Her pale-gloss lips bent up stiffly at the corners like wire.

"Such names do not fall to those of human lot."

A crease marred the smooth surface of her brow. "Confucius?"

"Close. Charlie Chan. Holly, maybe. Pride, possibly. Together they play like a conspiracy theory: Too tight, no flaws."

"Suppose I let your curiosity go on fluttering in the wind, how would that be?"

"Disastrous. My work's made up entirely of questions and answers. Who was it said if nothing's accomplished, no work was done?"

"Obviously not Congress. Just what *is* your business?"

"We settled that outside. Good-bye, Ms. Pride. It's been lovely." I turned and grasped the doorknob.

"Where are you going?"

"Where I started; Mr. Lawes's office. I think I can find it. It's not that big a suite, and I'm a trained detective. That's what you've been trying to find out, isn't it?"

"If you go prowling around, I'll have to call security. One of my responsibilities is to shield Fran — Mr. Lawes from annoying interruptions."

"My only responsibility is to see Francis — since we're being informal. I can't do that while I'm standing here talking in circles. I'm here by arrangement with him."

"Is it about Paula Lawes?"

I smiled. I'd gotten something out of the side trip after all.

"If he didn't tell you what it's about," I said, "it's not my secret to share." I opened the door, looking back over my shoulder. "By the way, is it congratulations, or good luck? Lawes gets one, you the other, but I'm fuzzy on the etiquette."

She glanced toward the picture on her desk. I still couldn't see who was in it, but now I didn't have to. "Who told you?"

"Observation and instinct, and one of those hunches that hardly ever pan out. The ring helped," I said, when she looked down at it. "But you're already asking the kind of questions a wife asks about her husband. He's picky when it comes to choosing a mate, if the pictures I've seen of Paula Lawes mean anything, and the kind of women he generally comes into contact with are in politics. The only really good-looking ones are in Hollywood, playing politicians. That leaves you and the blonde outside, who on short acquaintance has the personality of a paper clip."

"Impressive — and insulting to slightly more than half the world's population. You aren't much on people skills, Mr. Walker."

"It depends on which skills are required for the particular job. Good-bye again, Ms. Pride, and best wishes on your betrothal." I let myself out and pulled the door shut behind me.

SIX

No whistles blew and nobody tackled me as I walked past the receptionist's desk and stopped at the door facing the one that led into Holly Pride's office. The woman behind the desk didn't raise her chin from her smartphone, but I could feel her eyes following me from behind the glasses. This door was blank too. I knocked. A familiar voice asked who it was. When I identified myself, the owner of the voice invited me in. There was a puzzled frown in his tone.

"Why weren't you announced?" Lawes asked. He was sitting in front of a window in a padded leather chair, half-turned toward it with a hand resting on a paneled desk that might have stood next to Holly Pride's in the showroom. He had on the same dark gray suit and his beautifully brushed hair hadn't gone any grayer since morning.

"Ask your fiancée. She wanted to strip-search me before letting me into the royal presence."

"Holly told you we're engaged?"

"I told her. I had the impression she was the one who was pushing for your wife's declaration of death, but she put me straight on that when it took her a while to guess why I scaled the wall."

"You didn't get that impression from me. Holly knows nothing about it. I wanted to surprise her with the information that we were free to marry, when I have it. I wish you'd spoken to me first."

"So do I. When I get the third-degree, I'm used to getting it from a cop with b.o. Chanel Number Five throws me off my game."

"*Le Chat Blanc*'s her label," he said. "Seventy dollars an ounce. I gave it to her last Christmas. Now I'll have to spring for another bottle. I was going to give her the news for her birthday, if the timing worked out."

"From the look of her you'd have had to have it gilt-edged and engraved, with a diamond choker on the side."

Red spots the size of quarters blossomed on his cheeks. "Your lack of diplomacy goes beyond mere bluntness."

"You're not buying my diplomacy, Mr.

Lawes. I've just come from John Alderdyce," I said, shifting gears.

The spots didn't fade. "That son of a bitch. I should have filed a harassment complaint. If he'd spent half as much time looking for Paula as he did browbeating me, I wouldn't have had to hire you in the first place."

"As he saw it he was doing both. You didn't improve things by acting like you lost a favorite putter instead of your wife."

"I'd have bled from my palms if it's what he wanted. I deal with politicians, tycoons, lobbyists, and the press. It takes a poker face and a tough shell to bring them all together. I'm sorry if I don't fit the conventional profile of the distraught husband. I haven't that luxury."

"There is no conventional profile. I've seen psychopaths blubber real tears on cue and genuine victims stand up to ruthless grilling with all the outward emotion of a Roomba vac. But not many speak of their life partners in the past tense when they've only been gone a few hours."

"She'd been gone to me longer than that. Alderdyce might have mentioned what I told him at the time, that our marriage had been on automatic pilot for years. We neither loved nor hated each other; we just shared the same quarters. Neither of our careers gave us the time to file for separation or divorce. The Paula I spoke of in past tense was the Paula I fell in love with; *that* Paula was as dead as Cleopatra, as I suppose I was to her."

"There's also the small matter of a million dollars in death benefits. A cop looks at that and it's Christmas."

"A million, what's that today? In this office a year's worth of toner. I'm worth a million, probably more, and I spend what I must to get by and to put up just enough of a front to impress a client, but not so much he might think the city's gone back to business as usual. What would I do with another million, retire? Not today, and certainly not to smooth the ruffled feathers of the police."

"The police say you're up to your chin in debt."

He'd stopped to take in air. It had been quite an address to deliver in one breath. He found enough to snort; if that's what it's called in his tax bracket. "I've made satisfactory arrangements with my creditors. Is that all you've dug up since breakfast, the state of my finances and John Alderdyce's opinion of my character?"

"I broke for lunch."

He decided to get mad again; but I jumped

57

in before he could make another speech.

"I'm not paid to clean up messes, just sort them out. That takes time, especially when someone else got there before me and I have to figure out their system before I try mine. I came here to report and to collect photographs I can show around to jog the memory of people who haven't followed the case since it fell off the map."

That had a placating effect, for some reason; but then he'd built a business on giving just the right impression or no impression at all. In any case he spent some time watching cars cross town fifteen stories below his feet, his palm flat on the polished surface of his desk. When he lifted it to rub his chin it left no wet mark at all. He swiveled my way, opened and shut a drawer, and laid five pictures on the desk, fanning them out like playing cards.

I picked them up and shuffled through them. He took his women the way he took his mimosas, tall and cool. Paula had the somewhat rangy look of someone who knew her way around a bridle path. She didn't smile any more in hard copy than she had on his cell.

"One more question. Was Holly around when Paula disappeared?"

"Just what do you mean by that?"

"Questions never mean anything. Answers do."

"Yes. She was my receptionist then. It didn't take long to see she was overqualified for the job. Does that make her some kind of suspect?"

"Not according to the cops, or her name would've shown up in the paperwork."

"There'd be no reason. In those days our relationship was strictly professional."

"Thanks."

He watched me slide the pictures into a pocket. "Where are you going with them?"

"Allen Park, the last place your wife was seen. It seems as good a place to start as any."

"The trail started and ended there. What can you possibly hope to turn up that the police haven't, after all these years?"

"A crumb, maybe. A witness still in residence who didn't find talking to cops a good investment of his free time. A broken pencil point, red clay residue in a footprint in ordinary brown dirt; the usual stuff Miss Marple specializes in. A thread to tug at for want of a string."

"Are you sure you're not just running out the clock? I get enough of that from plasterers and electricians who work by the hour."

"Just clawing for traction, Mr. Lawes."

He showed his not-suspiciously-even teeth in ten centimeters of smile. "You switch metaphors like a yard engine."

"Work like one, too." Back and forth, forth and back. I left him.

My office building was under scrutiny for asbestos again. The subject came up every time it changed owners, and so far the solution had always been the same: Cover it up and hope the inspector doesn't notice or has a kid in college who can't catch a forward pass. It was no landmark, so it wasn't likely to be fobbed off on a syndicate based in Beijing like the others; but if the decision was to tear it down it would be all the same to me. Whatever they slung up in its place would be so swank and gaudy I couldn't get through the front door without a bulldozer. When they say Detroit's coming back, they don't mean you're coming with it.

The only sign the super was at his post was the odor of borscht boiling in his cubbyhole off the foyer. It followed me up two flights, where I pushed my door shut against the pressure. There the same old smell of dust and unintentional *pro bono* activity awaited me in the reception room. Sometimes a customer came straggling in to sneer at the magazines, serve a short stretch in Purgatory, then pass through the second door to unload the chains he'd forged in life; but not lately. I'd blame the Internet, but I'd been brick-and-mortar since Bill Gates was getting his shorts yanked down in gym and the traffic hadn't changed.

On into the holy of holies, where the feng shui was just as absent: two war-surplus file cabinets filled with dissatisfied clients and bills outstanding; a teacher's desk from a school since converted into a movie studio, then a crack factory, George Armstrong Custer selling beer from his crest in hell, long flaxen hair flying, saber flashing, buckskinned to the bone; all the details as accurate as a long-range weather report. Maybe that was the appeal. Not one of the cases I'd typed into the reports bore even a slight resemblance to what had actually happened, and I didn't consider myself a fabulist.

The only reason I'd stopped in at all was to check the mail, of which there was none under the slot, abuse my liver, and place calls on a secure landline; secure because I pose as much threat to authority as a sunken ship in a fishbowl.

I got out the photos of Paula Lawes and looked at them again, hoping to jump-start my powers of extra-sensory perception, but they weren't strong enough to turn over a new leaf. I put the pictures back in my pocket, drew out my notebook, and called the public relations firm she'd worked for. Three pickups and three music playlists later I got a sympathetic party who'd known her, liked her, and was willing to help with a new investigation into her vanishing act. I read off the list of her clients I'd gotten from the police file along with the rest of her known associates. Of the five I gave him, my new best friend said two had moved on, one was dead, but two were still customers, and would he like me to arrange interviews? I said not at this time, thanked him, depressed the riser, and dialed a number from the directory.

The voice I drew this time, buzzy like a telephone transmission in an old radio show, got everything out of me but my operation to correct a deviated septum before it agreed to relay my message to the person I wanted. I slobbered thanks all over the receiver and cradled it.

This season the stuff in the office bottle was burned only once, from a single source. I'd bought it out of the proceeds from a case that on second thought would have drowned better in Old Renal Shutdown. I pulled the cork — I think it was the sound of it that appealed — poured enough into a shot glass to float the dust, and rolled it between my palms to coax the bouquet up to my nostrils, like Highland heather marinated in nettle honey, or what I thought it would smell like.

That was almost enough. I might have poured it back into the bottle except it could contaminate the rest of the contents. I contaminated my stomach with it instead.

I let the telephone jangle three times before I picked up. The stuff was affecting me more than it used to, especially on a stomach lined with eggs Benedict, sourdough toast, pie a la muck, and Colombian sludge.

"A. Walker Investigations." I heard my voice drawing it out like a recovery crew dragging a pond for a corpse.

"This is Commander Albert White, retired. Who the hell is Amos Walker?"

It was a voice like my father's, ground to gravel shouting orders on a loading dock. "Someone who shares your initials," I said. "Didn't the party at headquarters give you the rest?"

"This is Allen Park. We've got no headquarters, just a police station. So you're conducting an investigation for a private party. I'm twice removed from that: Once, 'cause I'm retired. The second time, because when I *wasn't* retired I wouldn't give a private snog the temperature of my left nut. So why am I returning your call?"

"Why are you?"

" 'Cause it involves the Lawes case, and I'm sitting here on my back porch drinking fucking lite beer, pretending it's pilsner, black as Uncle Tom's ass and strong as a skunk's, and wishing I had another crack at it. How soon can you get here?"

"Commander White, that's me ringing your doorbell."

"When it is, make sure you're lugging a six-pack of Purple Gang."

SEVEN

The house was a fairly new brick ranch in a cul-de-sac off Outer Drive, with a straight-line view across the street to Detroit, specifically the VA hospital, an ugly sprawl of Lego-like construction where a line of ambulances waited outside the emergency room, eager to neglect their passengers.

A fluffy-looking woman of sixty in pea-green sweats answered the door and led me past a lot of wooden ducks, fishing creels, and Little Red Riding Hood baskets and out onto a screened porch, where a man sat in a wicker chair with a can of beer standing beside him on a cooler. The woman smiled and left us, walking noiselessly in blinding white sneakers.

Albert White hadn't changed much since his television interview the night Paula Lawes's car was found abandoned in his city. He looked just as flinty without the gaudy cap and stiff uniform, with steel-gray hair planed flat across the top of his head, eyes the same color set back in a web of sharp creases, a nose that had been broken and spliced, and a chin with a cleft you could park a bicycle in. He had on gray pleated slacks, brown shoes, and a pressed denim shirt. A bolo tie with a silver steer skull closed his collar.

He didn't stand or offer to shake hands, just snatched the six-pack I'd bought out of my grip and set it on the floor. "Warm as piss."

"They didn't have the brand in the cold case. Sorry."

"Grab a can." He removed his from the cooler.

I wasn't thirsty, and it was still a little chilly to be sitting on a porch drinking cold beer. Besides that it was lite; but I'd drunk worse under less pleasant conditions in the interest of establishing a bond. I tipped up the lid and dealt myself one from inside. A few more floated in slushy ice.

I reached inside my coat with my other hand and opened my ID folder, folding the honorary county deputy's star out of sight. It never impressed anyone anyway and would only put a real cop out of sorts. He waved a palm. " 'Course your name's Walker and you got a snooper's ticket. Who'd lie about that?"

Grinning, I put it away and sat in a wicker chair facing his at an angle. An above-ground pool stood in the backyard of the house next door, covered with a blue tarp and with the usual assortment of last summer's junk scattered around it, plastic lawn chairs and foam-rubber noodles, rust-stained by snow and rain and faded by sunlight. At that it was easier on the eye than the hospital.

"I heard John Alderdyce pensioned out," he said.

"If you want to call it a pension. It won't put his grandson through Michigan. He's filling the empty hours as a snooper."

"Damn shame. The state pays a football coach a million a year to wipe a freshman's ass but the city won't shake down dick to stand in front of a bullet. You know Detroit don't even foot the bill to bury an officer killed in the line of duty? The family has to pony it up on their own, or pass the hat like those pricks at the airport."

"What about Allen Park?"

"Oh, it's got a whole different set of rules in place to ass-fuck the boys and girls in blue." He sipped, lifting the can between thumb and forefinger, a delicate gesture that seemed uncharacteristic. "Who you working for?"

"Francis X. Lawes, the widower in the Paula Lawes case. If she's deceased. That's what he's paying me for, to confirm the vocabulary. He's got the wedding-bell blues and they won't wait."

"Risky, if the Detroit crew we dumped this one on weren't just guessing. They had him all ready to rope, tie, and brand — except for the rope and the tie and the iron."

"On the other hand, it goes a little way toward clearing him of murder. I don't buy the insurance angle; all he has to do is wait a year."

"On the *other* hand, it could be the ace he needs to play to get the system off his back. How many hands is that?"

"Too many. Anyone who's ever tried that 'why would I stick my head in a noose if I had anything to hide' act outside of cheap melodrama winds up stepping into the hole he dug."

"Not if he makes damn sure she'll never be found."

"You don't need a corpse in this state to prove murder. I might find something. I'm pretty good."

"Maybe he don't know that. That being the case, what's he figure he's got to lose?

You come up empty, he enjoys being single-o for another year — less, if I remember right — and gets married anyway. He's paying you to fall on your face and wash him in the blood of the lamb all at the same time."

"That's just about the opposite of what Alderdyce said. He thinks it's a dream job: deliver the goods in the way of evidence and put myself in a cozy spot with the cops. It wouldn't be the first time someone in their sights turned out to be too big for his skin."

"I hope he's right, if he's right about Lawes. The older I get the less I like living with the thought of another guilty bird flying free with the rest of the flock. When it comes to justice I'm just a sentimental old slob. Maybe it's why I hung it up."

"Is it?"

"Naw. I should've stopped at inspector. One rung closer to the chief is one rung too high. When the party in office changed I knew he'd be out on his ass and me with him, so I pulled the chain before they could. I'd never been fired from a job in my life and it was too late in the day to start setting precedents."

I drank beer. A gnat that had been tickling the back of my neck turned out to be something else. "Did you bone up on the

Lawes case after I called you?"

"Now, do I look like the kind of schoolboy that'd go on doing homework after he dropped out?"

"Looks don't count, you know that. You've worked a lot of investigations — plenty of them missing persons and homicide, I'm sure, working this close to Detroit. It was a high-profile beef, but a lot of soup's been spilled since. You're pretty strong on details after six years. You even know it's been a little more than six. Specific dates are just about the last thing anyone remembers, cops included."

A frown chiseled deep lines from the corners of his mouth to both sides of his chin. With the cleft in the middle, it looked as if he'd been scarred with a pickle fork.

"I wouldn't be likely to forget the very last case a good officer worked before some son of a bitch murdered him."

EIGHT

"You boys all right?" The screen door opened and the woman in sweats poked her fluffy head out onto the porch. She hadn't the reedy voice of an old lady; the timbre suggested vocal training. You never know about people based on appearance. We detectives are supposed to know that.

White switched his glare to her, then back to me. "Either of us laying on the floor grabbing his chest?"

"Well, you don't have to snap." The head withdrew and the door banged shut at the end of its spring.

"I'll pay for that." He sat back, swirling the beer left in his can. "Marcus Root, eight-year veteran, four commendations, one for dragging a five-year-old boy out of a retention pond and giving him CPR. The kid's a senior in high school now. When Paula Lawes's car was found abandoned, Root was the first responding officer."

71

I waited. Someone was playing scales up my spine.

"Same night," he said. "Well, the next morning, if you want to go by the clock. Busy tour. Observed a motorist driving erratically: tan late-model Chevy Impala. Plate muddy, couldn't radio the number while driving. His last report.

"Way the investigating team pieced it together, somebody pulled up alongside him and put two through the driver's window. Nine-millimeter slugs, closest thing to a brown paper bag in ballistics. One grazed his neck, the other went through his left cheek, exited out the right temple, and lodged in the headliner above the passenger door. His unit struck a lamppost. Witness found him slumped over the wheel. M.E. said he was dead before he hit the post."

"How'd it play out?"

"Didn't. We never found the Impala and nobody came forward to report what happened. We found everything on his person and in the car that was supposed to be there, except one thing."

"His notebook."

His empty can crackled in his grip. "You know? Sure, you came across that when you read up on the Lawes case. So why play Rain Man for me?"

"It was a guess. I'm a suspicious person. I didn't know about any cop-killing. Chances are the press didn't pick it up till the next day and it got lost in the glare of the other investigation. If I heard about it at the time I forgot."

"Yeah. PR flacks are always bigger scoops than a murdered cop. We're paid to be permanently in season."

"The first responder's report is the most important," I said. "He'd have given everything he had to the detective team while it was still fresh."

"You never held down a beat. The solid facts get set down first, for the record. Whatever thoughts, ideas, hunches, brainstorms come later, for the officer's own reference during debriefing. Some detectives don't like that: 'Kid, you wanna be Kojak, take the exam. Just for now, stick to what you saw and heard and save the fancy footwork for America's Funniest Felonies.' Me, I've only got one head, I can always use more. Only I didn't get it that time because he didn't live long enough to file the paperwork and whoever popped him ran off with his first impressions."

He finished crushing the can and threw it at a bucket half full of its ancestors. It struck the bail, bounced off, and rocked to a stop on the boards of the porch. "That's what kept me on the job long after Cynthia started nagging me to retire: some bottom-feeding, dick-licking, goat-fucking rat bastard going through a dead cop's pockets, handling him like he was a slab of meat after he killed him. I wanted that piece of shit so bad it made me piss blood every time I thought about it.

"Root had two little kids and a third on the way. Lost it when she got the news." He popped open another beer.

Mine had gone flat. I stood it on top of the cooler. "You think what happened to him had something to do with what happened to Paula Lawes?"

"He left Root's wallet alone, his service piece, the riot gun under the front seat. Why take his notebook if not for what was in it? Root hadn't worked anything worth a line in a weekly shopper in a month, and what he had before that was public record. Someone followed him from where her car was found, caught up to him while he was concentrating on a possible drunk behind the wheel, and capped him for what he had on paper."

"What made whoever it was so sure he had something that would come back on him?"

He paused with his can halfway to his lips. His face pitied me. "What made him sure it wasn't?"

"I don't like it," I said. "One side of it hangs together so well it stinks and the other falls apart based on sheer recklessness."

"Name one theory that doesn't."

"Leads?"

"We figured whoever snatched the woman had to have time to stash her someplace — her or her body — so he planted an accomplice at the scene to wait for the cops and do the rest. I never said either one of them was dumb. If she was taken it had to be fast, and fast can ball you up six ways from Tuesday; you can't expect to erase every possible incriminating detail in midstride. So you appoint somebody else to clean up, yeah?"

I nodded. It seemed the only appropriate response.

"Well, he'd better be good; both of 'em better. We had a gang operating here then, slick as eels. Started in drugs in Detroit, graduated to hired killing, splintered off into the suburbs when a new chief made gangs Priority One in the big city: You remember all those sweeps, seemed like there was one every Friday night and a matinee Saturday. Anyway the gang was in the catering business so long they made Murder Incorporated look like junior achievers. But that isn't the reason we lit on them first."

"Angle of the slug," I said.

"Grab another beer. You hit the bonus round. The vehicle it was fired from had to be riding low enough the bullet took an upward trajectory: thirty degrees, according to the lab monkeys in Detroit. First thing these gang-bangers do when they score a set of wheels is chop it so low when they drive over a dime they can read the date with their ass."

"And?" As if I didn't know the answer.

"And we made a sweep of our own. The impound looked like a convention-center parking lot in Scrote City."

Scrote was short for "scrotum." The language hadn't changed since I'd taken police training.

"Wasn't strictly wasted time," he said. "We bagged one for carrying without license or registration, two others for possession for sale of crack — three-time losers, the lot; Trifecta. Had a rape victim ID a fourth in a lineup. He's in the boys' school in Whitmore Lake till he turns eighteen in a year or so. Sweated the rest." He shook his head. "These pukes don't scare. To them the slammer's like graduation day, and if any of

76

'em lives to see thirty he'll get a block party."

"The gang leader still around?"

"Yeah, he's around." The next swig he took seemed to have given him lockjaw. He made a bitter face and threw that can after the last, slopping beer all the way. But this one landed in the bucket. "He's with the state police, Jackson post. Got him a steady job as a consultant on youth gang activity. That's how we enforce the law now. If you can't pin a rap on him, make it a badge."

I rested my palms on my thighs. I hadn't taken up his invitation to help myself to another brew. I was getting a contact high just watching him. "He sounds like he might be worth talking to."

"Why, because he switched sides? The only light Oakes Steadman ever saw came from the gold stud in his dick. He beat, killed, and raped his way to the top of the shitheap and stuck so long he got the attention of the other side. That's how we fight crime now: We make it legal."

Cynthia White — she could only be the retired commander's wife — let me out the front door without a trace of strain. That didn't mean Albert had ducked the bullet for that crack he'd made; when it came to the dodge, the rook, the Judas smile, a cop's wife can't be beat.

The sun bled over the western suburbs, leaving the river in shadow. I'd been at it all day and the farthest I'd gotten from that crooked stretch of water was the hour I'd spent in the library. I went home to count my losses.

The place needed a new roof, new windows, faucets that didn't drip, a more efficient furnace, and while we were at it an elegant mistress with an employee discount at Victoria's Secret. I parked in the garage, leaned shut the swollen door that led to the kitchen, and applied my investigative skills to the refrigerator.

Not much progress there either: a hard-boiled egg sealed in knockoff Tupperware, half a block of Velveeta, a bunch of wilted celery, two bottles of Heineken. The food didn't appeal to me and I sure as hell didn't feel like drinking any more beer. I smoked a cigarette for supper, scoured outer space for a TV program that wasn't as stale as the contents of my refrigerator, and mixed a highball; but I didn't drink that either.

Liquor hadn't been my friend lately. It made me drowsy, but it shook me awake the same time every night, after which I lay there for hours, fully alert, falling back to sleep finally just before the alarm rang. For several weeks now I'd opened my eyes in darkness, switched on the lamp, and the minute hand was always stuck just before or after midnight. It was so consistent I'd stopped looking.

So that night I laid off the booze, only to find myself conscious again two hours later. I swung my feet to the floor and sat there in my shorts, scrubbing my hair and taking inventory of all the things I regretted, as if the one that kept me from sleeping the night through would step up like a man and cop to it.

It didn't; but then again I may have overlooked it in the jumble. Couldn't be the latest, taking on a job that involved a missing person who'd stayed missing six years and change with two police departments looking for her, an organized band of psychopaths, and now a cop killing, just for garnish. The insomnia had been going on without help before I stepped into that pile of grief.

Just for laughs I looked at the alarm clock, standing in a moonbeam like the woman in white. Twelve o'clock on the nose.

NINE

It was a brand-new spring day in the Rust Belt. Gray clouds squatted on the roof, drooling a mix of rain and soupy, half-formed snowflakes. I drank a pot of coffee, smoked three cigarettes, and watched the slimy things licking streaks down the window over the sink. I was waiting for it to be eight o'clock.

A minute past I called the firm of Baylor, Schneider, Baylor, and Baylor. The fish I finally landed this time told me my helpful telephone acquaintance of yesterday was out. I read off the names of the two clients Paula Lawes had represented who were still with the service and asked if either was available.

"May I ask what it's about?" A female voice, clipped and brittle.

"You may."

The little silence that followed didn't do much for the quality of her tone. "I can't give you that information. Our clients' privacy is our number-one priority."

"Funny, I thought the purpose of public relations is to rescue them from too much privacy."

The voice got cautious. It hadn't been reckless to begin with. "Are you in the business?"

"I'm investigating a possible murder."

"Are you with the police?" She was practically whispering now.

"I'm working in cooperation with them." I'd always wanted to say that and mean it. It wasn't the thrill I'd expected.

Keys rattled. "Andrea Dawson's in a meeting in California. She won't be back until tomorrow. George Hoyle may be able to spare you some time. He works at home. I can call him."

I said so could I and pinky-swore not to invade his privacy. She gave me the number and hung up.

I entered the digits and counted the tones. Someone picked up just when the recording was due to come on offering repeat dialing.

"According to Hoyle."

I coughed to cover a moment's hesitation. "George Hoyle?"

"Yes?"

"My name is Amos Walker. I'm an independent investigator. They told me at your office you knew Paula Lawes. I've been hired to look into her disappearance."

He had one of those deep voices that could be warm or cold. It fell on the warm side. "I'm glad *some*body is. I hope I didn't throw you off with the way I answered the phone. It's the name of my business. That's the line you called."

"I got it from someone at Baylor etcetera."

"I bet you talked to Theresa. She's a company girl. When something strikes her as dicey she directs it away from the customers. No one can convince her it wouldn't mean a damn thing when it comes to trouble."

"Maybe the boss was eavesdropping. Where can we meet?"

"I'm not sure I'd be any help."

"So far my only contact who knew her personally is her husband. We're all of us different things to different people. You might have something to contribute that he couldn't."

"Here's good." He gave me an address in Harper Woods. That was a welcome change, as far inland as it was. Another day near the river and my mercury would be off the charts.

■ ■ ■ ■

You can spend a lifetime in metropolitan Detroit and never get to visit all the suburbs. They lie north, south, west, and east — if you count Windsor, which the Canadians would take issue with — and in some cases actually inside the city limits. Harper Woods sits just south of the Macomb County line, close enough to smell the swill from its county seat but far enough away to refresh itself with the scent of roses and good cocktails when the wind blows from Grosse Pointe. Somehow it manages to pack some twenty thousand souls into a piece of property about the size of a Home Depot without bruising any knees or elbows. But just where the woods went, nobody knows except the founding fathers.

George Hoyle lived and worked in two stories of more or less authentically Tudor-style house on a street with tree-plantings in the sidewalks, young enough to need gauze wraps to protect them from the wintry blend of snow and icy rain. The building was ivory-colored stucco with timbers stained mushroom gray and casement windows with real mullioned panes.

The place looked like money without shouting it.

The door chimes went bing-bong-bing-bong, bing-bong-bong-bing, the cadence of a bell in the steeple of a cathedral. The man who answered them had half an inch on me, making him six-one, with a long, handsomely seamed face topped with a pompadour of brown hair with gray in it. He was a five-dollar bill without the chin whiskers. He wore a white shirt open at the neck and rolled to his elbows, the tails neatly tucked inside gray corduroys. His feet were shod in black leather loafers slightly scuffed at the toes.

"Mr. Hoyle?"

"Yes. I'm afraid I've forgotten your name."

I reminded him. "What does According to Hoyle do?"

"We produce audiobooks."

"I used to listen to those sometimes. Not since they stopped recording them on tape. That's all I can play in my car."

"Pretty soon they won't be available on disc. MP-three's the latest twist in the race to avoid communication with the rest of our species. That's why I need public relations consultants, to assure each new generation I'm up to speed. The minute you start talking about tradition, you're sunk." He shook my hand. The fingers were corded and woody, like his voice and appearance. He let go and stepped aside, holding the door for me.

The living room would have provided Henry VIII with a pleasant transition into the twenty-first century: Heavy dark trestle-type tables, a lot of leather, an artificially faded and machine-moth-eaten tapestry mounted in a frame above the stone fireplace, and an iron chandelier equipped with bulbs in the shape of candles. Drops of fake wax adhered permanently to the sides of the sockets.

"Butt-ugly, isn't it?" he said. "I'm subleasing from an interior decorator. She's in Santa Fe, polluting movie stars' homes with clay pots and Mexican tile. The only reason I took it is she had a spare studio I could convert into an editing room."

I followed him down a short hall lined with dim portraits of women in ruffled collars and men in codpieces, and we turned into a small room containing a control board and monitors. It resembled the technician's space at WDIV, but instead of pictures the screens displayed a series of jagged lines like in a business chart, frozen in place. He closed the door. It was upholstered with some kind of fabric that had not been grown anywhere outside a test tube, shutting off all the ambient sounds from the rest of the house. Snow and rain slobbered steadily past a triple-paned window in complete silence. A bomb could have gone off in the little side yard and you'd never know it if you didn't happen to look up and see the flash.

"Excuse me just a moment," he said, seating himself in an office chair, the bare bones type covered in padded gray vinyl. "This reader's okay, but . . ." He trailed off, flipping a pair of switches and twisting a dial. A voice nearly as deep as his issued from an invisible speaker, stirring the jagged slashes on the monitors with each change in pitch.

". . . memories, which are my life — for we possess nothing certainly except the past — were always with me. Like the pigeons of St. Mark's, they were everywhere, under my feet, singly, in pairs, in little honey-voiced congregations, nodding, strutting, winking . . ."

He squashed his thumb on a key. The voice stopped, the oscilloscope (or whatever it was) readings stood still on the screens. "There! Did you hear it?"

"The voice sounded familiar."

"It should, for what I pay him. Hang on." He touched the key again, then the one left of it; paused again, and replayed what we'd heard. I turned my better ear — the one opposite my shooting hand — toward the source. This time I heard it. The consonants at the end of the phrase "in little honey-voiced congregations" were crisp and tweedy. At, "nodding, strutting, winking," they lost shape. I said, "He went from London to L.A. in one jump."

"Exactly. Prick forgot the British accent. It wasn't great to begin with, but at least up to this point he didn't sound like a Beverly Hills cabbie. The floor manager should've caught it at the time and done another take. The customers pick up on such things; plucks 'em right out of the story. Now I have to go back and listen straight through four hours of boring English country shit to find out how many times he dropped the bloody ball."

"Tish-tush. That's no way to talk about Evelyn Waugh."

He turned his attention from the board. "A detective who reads. Now I know you're not with the police."

"You'd be surprised. Just yesterday I heard a detective in Major Crimes say 'whom,' and she used it correctly. What are you going to do to this guy, stick him behind Traitors' Gate?"

"As much as Waugh might approve — which if you know anything about the old crank, you wouldn't be so foolish as to expect it — I can't. This clown makes twenty million a picture. Someone might miss him. So I have to schedule another studio session, work my way around his busy shooting schedule, get the publisher to go halfsies on his first-class plane ticket and eat the cost of his mountain-grown chamomile tea and Caesar salad — dressing on the side and hold the anchovies — and maybe break even on sales, if anyone reads classical literature anymore. Can't count on that, so we wheedle box-office favorites into pimpery. Never mind that their particular gift doesn't necessarily transfer to this medium. Sure doesn't in this case."

He scribbled digits from a small LED screen on the control board onto a pad. The gizmo seemed to be an odometer of some kind. "When the publishers don't kick I use professional readers. They use a different tone for every character: men, women, foreigners, English majors, gutter rats. You never have to rewind to know who's speaking. In the golden age of radio they'd be major stars. As it is they make the industry minimum."

"On the plus side, no one hounds them

for their autograph in a public toilet. Can we talk about Paula Lawes?"

"Before we do that, can I see something that says you're who you say you are?"

I got out my folder and snapped it open. "Don't pay attention to the badge," I said. "It's pure milk chocolate under the foil."

He shook open a pair of black-rimmed glasses, put them on, and read the works, including the sell-by date. He returned the readers to his shirt pocket and the folder to me. "I'm forced to be suspicious," he said. "When you run a business from your home, of course you have a safe. I don't; but try telling that to a certain class of people." Without looking he slid a drawer under the control board open far enough to show the curved walnut grip of a revolver.

"Someday they'll stop printing cash and then we can all hang up our weapons for monuments." My coat spread open as I was putting away the folder, just enough to show the fisted rubber grip of the Chief's Special in its clip.

His face scowled from forehead to chin, which was a long way to stretch a scowl. "You can stop quoting the classics now. Just because you know Shakespeare and Waugh from Smith and Wesson doesn't mean you can find my Paula."

TEN

There was a faint smell of cigarettes in the house. Probably there were ionizers in place to scrub the air, but the odor was getting to be rare indoors, so I noticed it, along with a shallow glass ashtray on top of the control board. I showed him my pack and lifted my brows. He nodded, accepted one of the two I shook out, and I lit us both up. No one ever dropped a spent match into a tray with more care. "*Your* Paula?"

"That's right." He blew it out with the smoke. His face was something I could shoot pool on.

"How long?"

"Six months, two weeks, three days."

"Lawes know?"

"I have no idea. I was able to account for my whereabouts the night she disappeared. The Detroit inspector in charge of the case promised me it wouldn't get into the record unless it bore on the investigation. I forget his name."

"John Alderdyce. He's retired now."

"Apparently he's a man of his word. Nobody with the press ever tried to contact me. Frankly, the reason I agreed to see you is I wanted to know if I was going to be dragged into the business after all."

"I can make the same promise. Did you and Paula ever meet in Allen Park?"

He dragged on his cigarette deeply enough to burn it halfway down. The smoke stuttered out between his lips like steam escaping from a pressure valve. "So I have to clear myself with you as well."

"I've known Alderdyce most of my life. If he's satisfied, that goes for me too. That town is so far on the other side of the tonier suburbs — geographically and culturally — it's made-to-order for hookups after hours. The likelihood of either of you running into someone you know is so small a thimble could hold it. If she went there to meet you, she might have gone there to meet others."

"So one word from me and she's a slut." He ground out the butt in the glass tray. "I don't think we're going to get along after all."

"My work isn't white-collar, Mr. Hoyle. I get a lot of grease under my nails and I don't make many friends. I've read the reports, I brushed up on the press coverage. Anything I might say or think has already been said out loud. The difference between cops and the press is the police try to keep it in the family while the people who are supposed to report the news use it to sell papers, goose up ratings, and elect friends. If there were anything to it beyond speculation — anything that could be attributed — it would still come up every time the story gets a fresh transfusion. I don't have anything to sell except answers. It's what puts the private in private detective."

"Sure. Forget I said anything. Are you a drinking man?"

"On rainy days."

We returned to the living room, where I sat on brown distressed leather with bulbs flickering in a chandelier eight feet overhead, pretending to be candles. The room made me want to gnaw on a mutton joint and wash it down with mead. Instead I accepted a whiskey sour in a highball glass and clinked it against his. He ditched his latest cigarette in a saucer on the trestle coffee table, settled into an upholstered torture rack of a chair, and sipped.

"Go ahead," he said. "Start turning the spit."

I swallowed good bourbon and crossed

my legs. "Nothing like that. Alderdyce has made up his mind Lawes killed his wife."

"Not because of Paula and me. The inspector himself decided that in the end, or he wouldn't have sat on what I told him about us. Also Lawes was too cold a fish to work up what's needed to commit a crime of passion."

"You know him?"

"Met him just once, at a Christmas party Baylor threw for clients and staff; he was Paula's plus-one. I'm an editor, which makes me a fair judge of character by profession. It didn't take me more than one cup of eggnog to get his number."

"Alderdyce agreed, which is why he cleared you in the end. He's got it worked out as a straight case of murder for money. The Lawses had life insurance policies on each other to the tune of a million apiece."

"He must be worth several times that."

I plucked the lemon twist from the lip of my glass and laid it in the ceramic plate; it tickled my nose, and spoiled the effect of the liquor. "Net worth's complicated," I said. "It can be all tied up in real estate in a seller's market, mortgages, bonds set in concrete till they're ripe. Also just because you've got a bundle doesn't mean you can't use more; even Lawes admitted that. It's an old cop standby, very convenient. And most of the time it happens to be right."

"So why did you take the job?"

"I think this time it happens to be wrong. When rich people need money, they almost always need it fast. Why rig it so her body was never found? Insurance companies don't pay on spec. He'd have to have known that without solid evidence of her death the process would take years."

"That's what you do, clear the innocent?"

"Only when it pays."

He smiled for the first time; drank off the top of his whiskey. "I'm glad you said that. Idealists make me nervous: so intent on do-ing only the right thing they wind up doing nothing. You know the Gamesman Inn?"

"No."

"There's no reason you should. I'm not even sure it's still there. It advertised itself as a sports bar, but the big-ass monitors were just for show, to keep the bluenoses from picketing out front. The screens were set just high enough on the walls to keep the rest of the room in darkness. They gave the local cops a discount so they didn't decide to bust the place anyway for complic-ity in immoral activities. There's a state law still on the books prohibiting extramarital sex."

"Like the one requiring motorists to engage a pedestrian to walk in front of automobiles waving a red flag."

"Right. It costs less to ignore those than to take them off the books. You never know when some D.A. might decide to dust one off, either to nail someone he couldn't otherwise or bring it to light to disgrace the other party when it's in office. Anyway it was the place to go in Allen Park when you get tired of meeting in backseats and no-tell motels."

"That where you and Paula went?"

"I didn't say that. I'm just telling you it exists."

I lit a cigarette, to give me an excuse to pull a face. "How do you think my job works? If I go there, assuming it still exists, and show Paula's picture around, I'm going to ask who she was with. The idea is to find out who else she might have been seeing who had a better reason than you to keep the thing quiet, but if anyone remembers that far back, your description might come up."

"You really think anyone will?"

"No. If the joint survived, and on the meager possibility that anyone who worked there then is still on staff, the odds of picking out one face from the thousands who have passed through in the meantime are worse than tapping the lottery. But records don't always get thrown away, and if someone who met her there was dumb enough to use a credit card . . ."

"Okay, since none of that's going to happen. What do you want to know — aside from the details you won't drag out of me with a tow chain?"

"This. Did anyone — a waiter, a bartender, or a customer — show any sign of recognizing her when you were there together?"

He frowned into his drink. "No. It's been — well, one thing. I told you cops stopped there sometimes, because of the break on the bill."

He hadn't said that, exactly; but I nodded.

"One night — I think it was the last time we went there — a group of local police officers was drinking at the next table. One of them spotted us and came over. I seized up; thought maybe he was some red-hot looking to enhance his arrest record or shake us down. But he spoke only to Paula, leaning a hand on the back of her chair."

A bad molar that had been in hibernation lurched awake, stabbing me to the bone. It was as if I'd bitten down on tinfoil. Sudden insight is seldom pleasant to the senses. I jumped, brushing cigarette sparks from the front of my coat.

He didn't appear to have noticed. "I couldn't hear the conversation," he said. "The place had a low ceiling, trapped all the jabber from the tables and the monitors — but he called her Paula and she smiled that tight little noncommittal smile of hers and said something back. I think she called him —" His face screwed up. "Mark? No; Marcus, I think. Yes. Marcus. No last name, of course. She didn't introduce us."

"Root," I said. "Marcus Root. Someone shot him to death the night Paula went missing."

II
REMEMBERING
MARCUS

ELEVEN

He played with his drink while I gave him what I'd gotten from ex-Commander Albert White, rolling the glass between his palms in the wet circle it'd made on its cork coaster.

"He ruled out coincidence?" he asked when I'd finished.

"I've never seen the word on a police report, and I've read thousands. I'm not sure any cop ever bothered to learn how to spell it."

"Because if the driver of that Impala he was following shot him, he probably wouldn't take time to read Root's notebook to see if he'd written anything down that would tie him to it. He'd just grab it and go."

"Granted. White's got a mad on for that youth gang. Either he couldn't let go of it or thought he could use the shooting for a catchall to break it up. Nothing lights a fire

101

under a police department like a cop-killing."

"You sound convinced."

"I'm not convinced the Big Dipper will come out at night until I see it. I think I'll check out this bird Steadman and see what he's got to say."

"Give up on the Gamesman?"

"Did you tell Alderdyce about it?"

"Sure. I got the impression if I held anything back he'd sniff it out, and there it'd all be on the official record."

"You got the right impression. Anything the staff and clientele could have to offer he'd have gotten out of them at the time. I try not to stretch the expense account covering ground the Detroit Police Department has already scraped clean. Did you tell him about the cop dropping by your table?"

"No. He didn't ask the question you did, and I didn't think of it at the time. If I ever did afterwards, it didn't seem important. How come you thought to ask and he didn't?"

"If I knew how to read his mind, I might be retired myself, with a pension from the city. At a guess I'd say he was working a different angle. When a case is this old, you grasp at whatever flotsam may still be bobbing about."

He stopped rolling the glass and took a sip. The face he pulled told me he'd regretted warming it up. He set it down with a thump and pushed it away. "You know, *this* is the kind of murder I could see being committed by the Francis X. Lawes I met that one time. No emotion involved."

"Didn't Paula ever talk about him?"

"No, apart from the fact there wasn't a great deal of affection in the marriage; that's kind of important territory in cases of — well, what we were involved in. 'My husband doesn't understand me,' that sort of thing. That's boilerplate, wouldn't you think? In her way she was as tight-fisted about personal history as she seemed to be in general."

"So it was just sex between you."

"That's a hell of a cold-blooded way to put it. We were both lonely. Let's leave it at that."

I finished my drink and put it down. "No soap. I'm no good at it. But if it turns out to be the missing piece I need, I'll come to you with it first. If it doesn't break another way."

"Now you sound just like Alderdyce."

"Thanks — for taking the time." I stood, shook his hand, and left him to deal with Evelyn Waugh and Joe Hollywood.

The slushy mess had settled into sullen rain. My head was a balloon. I blamed the bourbon. Scotch comes by sea; the cradling influence gentles it down. On the other hand, I wasn't aging as well as the bottled in bond. I guided the Cutlass into a lot next to a chain steakhouse, where I sponged up the poisons with a medium-rare sirloin, baked potato, and a demijohn of caffeine.

Twenty minutes later, synapses sparking, I let myself into my waiting room, just to punch in, check the mail, and go through the motions of maintaining office hours. I hadn't had any street traffic all year, but if you let one thing slip you can wind up living in sweats and eating over the sink.

Which wouldn't happen today. I had a customer.

She stood with her back to me, studying the framed *Casablanca* poster on the wall to the left of the coffee table with its selection of tired magazines. Some people are as identifiable from behind as when you're facing them, even on brief acquaintance. Today it was a linen slack suit, mocha-colored, with matching steeplejack pumps strapped by some engineering feat to her heels. Her short hair was as white as refined sugar, tapering to a point two inches above an ivory silk collar. Her weight rested on her right leg, shooting her hip. Her crossed arms squared off her shoulders with the precision of an architect's drawing.

"Is it original?" A gold-flecked brown eye gazed back over a shoulder.

"Early re-release. I got it from a client who came up short in the divorce. I haven't started accepting livestock yet."

Holly Pride turned around. Her bangs were still slanted. Embroidered braided vines canted down the left side of her blouse, same color as the fabric, following the line of the gorge of her jacket. She was a fan of acute angles.

She frowned at my reaction. "You don't approve?"

"It's better than yesterday; but then we're only on the third floor. I think I can get through this without Dramamine."

"You talk as if I made an appointment."

"If you did, would I be late?"

She glanced down at the tiny octagonal face of a gold watch on her wrist. "Probably. You should hire a receptionist if you can't be here during office hours."

"An intern, once. I caught him making for the door with the poster. I can barely afford to pay my own salary. Let's go into the isolation booth." I jingled my keys.

She came in past me as I held the door, glanced at the furnishings without comment, and sat in the customer's chair, resting her elbows on the arms and crossing her legs. A tiny blue tattoo winked at me from the little depression between the protruding bone of her left ankle and the Achilles tendon. I couldn't make out what it was without staring; but I was curious.

"Have you made any progress?" she asked when I sat facing her across the desk.

I smiled. "Can you believe it's the middle of April? What's the global warming crowd got to say?"

"So we're going to go through that again."

"Last year it was La Niña. Now it's El Niño. Next year, who knows? What Mexican family ever stopped at two kids?"

"His interest in this case is mine. Withholding from me is the same as withholding from your client. That's unethical. Just what are you grinning about?"

"Was I? I'll stop." I reached up and touched my mouth. "Nope."

"Did I say unethical? I should have said slimy."

"Does this approach work with Francis? Maybe. I guess even the Pope sheds his bulletproof vest at the door."

Coral nails rattled on the wooden chair

106

arm. She uncrossed her legs and recrossed them the other way. I tried to get a better look at the tattoo, but she was too fast. "You know this investigation will lead nowhere. What if I let you off the hook? What do they call it? A kill fee?"

"Does Lawes know you're here?"

"I don't have to file a flight plan when I'm on my own time."

"You won't mind if I call him and ask if he objects to your paying me off to walk away?" I picked up the telephone.

She rolled a shoulder. Her diamond-shaped chin was firm. I started pressing keys. A trim hand darted out and closed over mine. I cradled the receiver and sat back.

She did the same. I got a glimpse of the tattoo then: a thistle, prickly with sharp thorns. I hadn't expected a rosebud. Her nails rataplanned again. "What if you find Paula's remains? Because I'm sure that's all she is, a bundle of bones. The police would reopen the investigation, come to the same conclusion as before, which is no conclusion at all, and meanwhile Francis' name would be dragged through the mud worse than before. It would ruin him professionally. It wouldn't matter if he were cleared publicly. Our court system carries no provision for proving innocence. What politician would continue to employ someone who's been the prime suspect in a murder?"

"You should be making this speech to Lawes. As he sees it, I'm his wedding gift to you."

"If he'd discussed it with me before he spoke to you, I'd have asked him to buy me a pair of earrings instead. What's another eleven months out of a lifetime together?"

"Put it to him that way. If he buys it, he can call me off over the phone. My time's already paid for."

"You don't know him the way I do. Once he gets his teeth in something he never lets go."

"Something tells me yours is a match made in heaven, Ms. Pride. You wouldn't have another reason for wanting me off this one, by any chance?"

"Such as?"

"Such as you were there when his wife dusted. Maybe you know something you think nobody else does and that it might jump up and smack your fiancé in the face."

"And what might that be?"

"If it's Paula's affair with George Hoyle, you can relax. The cops know all about it and have dismissed it as a motive for murder."

A line of emotions crossed her face. It was like watching a magic-lantern display. When she got to anger it stopped. She scissored her legs and stood. "I should throw something at you for that."

"Better not. I'm a little fragile. You could break me with a block and tackle."

As curtain lines went it wasn't that good, but she took it to the exit. I heard her heels clicking down two flights of stairs, but I wasn't really listening. The first of the emotions that had swept her from ear to ear was relief. I'd thrown a dart in the dark and hit the bull square in the eye. I just wished I knew what to do with it.

TWELVE

"Michigan State Police, Jackson post."

I introduced myself to the owner of the crisp female voice and asked if Oakes Steadman was available.

"Hang on."

I listened to Barry Manilow for three minutes. Then a shallow, boyish voice came on the line. "Gang Unit, Steadman."

I gave him my name and said I was cooperating with the Detroit Police in a homicide investigation.

The voice lost some of its youthful quality. "Who says I ever had anything to do with Homicide?"

"Albert White. He's retired from the Allen Park Police."

"You said Detroit."

"Murders don't get committed in any of the suburbs without Detroit stepping in."

"I've got a clean ticket, mister. I'm with the good guys now."

"I'm not accusing you of anything. This murder I'm investigating may or may not be connected to the killing of an Allen Park police officer the same night."

"Marcus Root."

I scratched my ear. "That came pretty quick for something that happened more than six years ago."

"You don't forget getting dragged out of bed on no charge and grilled for three days without a break."

"You could have sued the city."

"I could of got shot in front of the courthouse and woke up in the morgue with a throwaway piece in my hand. What you think I decided?"

"Did you know Root?"

The laugh that got was as old as Pike's Peak. "Know him? I could practically claim him as a dependent on my taxes."

I looked at the beer advertisement in its frame. Custer leered back at me from his hill. "If that means what I think it does, we should finish this conversation in person."

Cars crawled bumper-to-bumper along I-94. The drivers were working up a fine rage to take home to the spouse and kids. After two hours I bailed out at Michigan Avenue and joined the parade lock-stepping

111

from light to light. It wasn't much faster but the scenery was better, at least until I entered the city limits.

Jackson's a prison town, and even though the old state penitentiary became a tourist trap after its last inmate, a former Detroit mayor, got transferred to a facility out West, the place still smells of the can. Pawnshops, check-cashing services, and bail bondsmen thrive around the crumbling skyscrapers in its center, and the crime rate's one of the highest in the country.

The billboard advertising the Imperial Massage Parlor featured a Manga-type geisha with eyes the size of planets and red lips big enough to French-kiss Godzilla. The woman who answered the bell of the frame house was four-feet-six and seventy pounds of crumpled parchment in a dress made from a grocery sack. Seals from all the local lodges decorated the door frame and the smell of boiled cabbage coming from back in the building swam thick as chowder. Most of the rub-a-dub joints in the New World have Japanese names and all-Korean staffs.

"Oakes Steadman," I said.

The leer she put on for customers vanished and she stood aside to let me enter. Foot traffic had worn a ditch in the linoleum, leading to various rooms sealed with heavy blackout curtains.

My hostess stopped short, throwing an arm across me in protective grandmotherly fashion. A porcelain doll wearing only a short silk kimono swept out of one of the curtained rooms directly in front of us, carrying something in a makeshift sack fashioned from a terry towel, and let herself through a door at the end of a short hallway. She left a trail of jasmine, or what I supposed jasmine would smell like.

"Hair crippings." The ancient Asian woman lowered her arm and we resumed walking.

I said nothing. English gave me enough challenges without trying to learn her lingo.

The house was larger than it looked from the front. It had probably started out around a thousand square feet, then built onto over the years in a shotgun arrangement, back and back as far as the plot and the local zoning laws would allow.

I breathed through my mouth and followed her down another dim hallway with the cabbage stench growing stronger until it smacked me in the face in a kitchen designed in Early John Travolta: A man could succumb to avocado poisoning just looking at the major appliances. A six-quart pressure cooker stuttered steam with an angry hiss on one of the stove burners. The smell made me crave corned beef on rye.

The old woman knocked on a door opposite the entrance. A voice came from inside and she opened the door, inclining a head of dishwater-gray hair toward the room beyond.

Actually it was a suite, or whatever you call a spacious apartment laid out on an open plan, without walls except for one containing a half-open door with gleaming gray-pink porcelain beyond, a modern-looking bathroom. The place was even less well lighted than the hallway, by a couple of table lamps with dark shades. I paused inside the door to wait for my pupils to catch up.

A throat cleared, a harsh sound that was nearly a growl. I took a step back to get a better look at the biggest Oriental I'd ever seen.

We're not supposed to call them that anymore, but this one was straight out of history. I'd seen him, and his twin, in a print in a book, flanking a withered emperor on a throne, with scimitars on their shoulders. It was from a painting made by a Westerner who'd managed to smuggle himself into and out of the Forbidden City without feeding the rats in the imperial gardens. You read some funny stuff when you spend a lot of time on stakeout, watching people come and go.

Actually, he was the biggest *anything* I'd seen apart from a porch post. He was nearly eight feet tall. If he stood on tiptoe he could punch his head through the popcorn ceiling. The ceiling would get the worst part of that deal; the head was helmetlike, the hairless scalp stretched taut over solid bone, canting back in flat planes at the temples, and sat atop a neck mortised and tenoned to his shoulders.

South of that he was less impressive, except for one feature, the gun in his right hand. His faded blue T-shirt clung to a hollow chest and his upper arms were no bigger around than his wrists, making his hands look as large as platters. The gun was a chromed .44 magnum. It was the size of a sickle, but it fit the fist that held it, although its weight made his wrist droop. His legs were thin too in green cargo pants, ending in feet that would enter every room five minutes before the rest of him. His sneakers would come custom by way of the NBA.

"Gigantism."

This came from a corner of the room I'd thought was uninhabited until my eyes adjusted to the gloom. Oakes Steadman — it had to be him — leaned against a wall with his arms folded. He was a well-built thirty in a white dress shirt rolled to his elbows, Wranglers artfully torn at the knees, and boots that laced to the ankles. The whites of his eyes glistened against mocha-colored skin and black dreadlocks hung to his shoulders.

"That's the word you hear," he went on. "Probably it's obsolete, like 'midget,' but Py don't mind so I ain't looked it up. Something in the glands. His parents was normal pocket-size slants."

The revolver was getting to be too much for the big man. He reached across his body and gripped his right wrist with his left hand for support. While he was busy with that I kicked him in the shin. The gun thumped to the floor and he followed it down, landing on his backside. The jar wasn't loud enough to be heard in Toledo.

I bent to pick up the magnum, but I didn't get that far. The black semi-automatic that appeared when Steadman unfolded his arms was only a fifth of the size of the .44, but the hand that held it didn't seem likely to let go of it as easily.

THIRTEEN

"You didn't have to do that," he said.

"I thought I did; though he folded easier than expected."

"Py's for show only. I'm supposed to tote a gun-carrier around with me. This could put me in cold storage." He rattled the pistol. "Our little secret?"

"Cross my heart. Py's my only corroborating witness."

He looked down at the big man. Py didn't look so much like the front row of the Terra-Cotta Army now; more like a skinny Buddha. He sat there with his jaw hanging, a poster boy for Mongolism.

"They grow too fast for strength to keep up. Don't live long, neither. He's almost at the limit. He's no use to me for a week now. I wisht you hadn't done that."

"You said."

"Healed?"

Moving glacially, I spread my coattails and

turned around. Establishments like that usually come with somebody who knows what to look for in a customer.

"Let's see you're who you said you were on the phone."

I broke out the folder and tossed it to him. He caught it with his free hand — the gun stayed steady — and flipped it open. His lips moved when he read, but that could be just for show, like his pet freak. He tossed it back. "That tin star could cost you your license."

"It wouldn't fool a kid. I only keep it for the weight." I put it away. When I looked back at him the pistol had vanished. "Why the dumb show? If I was going to brace you it wouldn't be here on your home court."

"I can't afford to count on that. You could be a friend of Marcus Root's; or a friend of an old enemy. I got 'em up to the chin from both sides of the fence."

"That why you don't hang out in the state police post?"

He didn't answer that one. "Py's uncle owns this crib, along with a dozen others between here and Grand Rapids." He tilted his head toward the big revolver where it lay on the floor. "Put it on the table, but don't get any cute ideas. It ain't loaded, and I filed down the firing pin just in case. He's clumsy enough to sneeze and jerk the trigger."

I hoisted it and laid it on the nearest lamp table, glancing at the chambers as I did so. They were empty.

He reached over to the lamp near him. It had a three-way switch. When he took it up to the limit, the objects in the room assumed shape. I cranked up the lamp on my side. An orange shag rug covered the floor, most of its nap squashed flat and as grimy as a rug in student housing. The tables and two unmatched armchairs screamed garage sale. The wallpaper was flocked and discolored. "Homey," I said. "Where'd you shop, Bed, Bugs and Beyond?"

"I had a better layout in the Wayne County lockup, but here I get to go out Saturday night. I can't beef about the rent. Old Man Chung puts me up to cut down on raids. Also I keep his boy out of trouble. He's a walking target."

"How can he be sure you aren't casing the place so the cops know where to look?"

His smile was tight-lipped, and gave out short of his eyes. They were opaque, like the skin that forms on a bowl of soup. "I'm with the cops, but I'm not a cop. It carries certain benefits. I'm gonna give up free room and board because a back rub turns into a hand job or better, customer gets his change in the form of a Ziploc bag full of 'ludes?"

Py's electrolytes had begun to blink back on. The eyes half-hidden under the epicanthic fold shot poison darts at my face, but he didn't stir from the floor. Steadman scooped up the magnum, leaned down, and held it out to him butt-first. The big man snatched hold of it like a dog snapping at a treat and held it loosely across a thigh thinner than my own.

"How'd you get this gig?" I asked Steadman.

"I done a nickel up in Marquette for GTA" — grand theft auto — "had me a reunion there with some bangers I hadn't saw for a while. They was all talking about who they was gonna get even with when they got out, what new skids they'd work, same old shit I heard all the time in the boys' school, some of it from the same mouths. None of 'em figured to last long enough to buy liquor legal. Me, I like it here above ground. I started staying away from 'em, playing the house nigger for the turnkeys, helping some fresh fish learn what their teachers didn't bother to pass on to them when they was in school. After two years a social worker came in and gave me an IQ test; turns out I got enough going up above my eyebrows to get my GED and even take a crack at college if I want. So the warden gives me a pass to use the computer room and in two months I ain't a dropout no more.

"I guess Lansing keeps tabs on my kind of case, 'cause four months before my parole I get a registered letter from a state police commander to come in for an interview when I walk out; he even offers to put in a word with the board during my review. Since the city cops think the way to solve the gang problem is run a sweep twicet a year, tag a few, and turn the rest loose, the governor hands it over to the troopers. I'm an inside expert. So here I am, a high school honor-rollee with what you might call a full ride scholarship with the University of Scrote Studies."

"Now you sound like Albert White."

He looked ready to spit. "That old piece of shit. He'd like me to go down for Root. That'd make it worth all the wires he pulled to make that crook look like Jesus."

"Tell me about Root."

"Slot machine. You fed in the right coin, next time you got caught up in a sweep, whatever you might be carrying in your jeans didn't make it into the evidence room. That way, if you fell short, there was plenty of shit to choose from when you wasn't carrying."

"Anyone ever file a complaint?"

"Bangers was all he muscled. They're gonna bop into the cophouse, ax Officer Leathernuts to take down their statement? That ain't the kind of suicide they got in mind."

"Any evidence?"

"I give a shit you don't believe me? You called me. I didn't issue any invitations."

"White thinks there's a connection between Root's death and the Lawes disappearance. Root was the first officer on the scene. White as much as said your gang took the job on a hire to seal his mouth. Whoever killed him took his notebook."

Steadman's face flattened. "I wasn't deaf, and I didn't have no reason then to pass anything along any ideas I had. Root wasn't popped over that deal, or if he was it was a twofer. He swallowed the bait set out to take him off a lot of guys' backs."

"The Impala."

That, according to White, was the car Root was getting ready to pull over when he was killed.

"A little water on the plate and a drive down a dusty road, and the heap could belong to the queen of England for all you could make out the numbers," he said. "I used to hunt pheasants in empty lots in Detroit. When a female's nesting, she staggers off faking a busted wing to draw you away from her chicks: Same thing when you drive like a drunk. The most experienced cop in the world don't see nothing else but that."

"Not even a low-rider pulling up alongside him with a shooter in the passenger seat."

"Just a guess, like I said."

The man on the floor had decided to get up. He stuck the muzzle of the magnum against the floor and used it as a pry. It was no way to treat an expensive firearm, even an inoperable one, but with the leverage he might have gotten himself upright sometime before sundown. I grew bored with the show and returned my attention to Steadman.

"Why snitch Root's notebook? It couldn't identify anyone connected with his murder, if that's how it went down. He wouldn't have been writing in it while he was getting ready to flag a driver."

"I ain't got nothing for that. This the first I heard it was ripped off. Must of been one of them things the cops sit on to prune back the phony confessions." He rolled a shoulder. "Probably it was somebody being cute. When you're looking for a notebook, maybe you're not looking so hard for a man."

"Not if you're a cop, and the man you're looking for killed one of your own."

"I said it was cute. I didn't say it was smart. What'd I say about them pukes and the future?"

"You wouldn't happen to remember how you came by your theory."

"Uh-uh. It's getting to be a long time ago, and I was daydreaming is all."

I couldn't read anything in his expression. A civilian has to earn eyes like those; just one killing won't do it. Cops have them, too, but for all I know they bring them with them to the academy. It isn't one of those jobs you drift into.

FOURTEEN

I actually started to ask the next question that came to mind. I covered it with a cough, and put out my latest cigarette, as if that was the cause.

Half of detection — the half that's easiest on the legs — is asking questions and getting answers. Even if they're lies it's progress of a kind. Nothing types a character like the falsehoods he chooses to employ. But sometimes the questions left unsaid are the wisest. It isn't like conducting a radio interview, where silence is a problem. A pause in the flow of an interview can be as good as a breakthrough, if you knew how to work it. Someday I hope to learn how. I thanked him for his time and turned toward the door. A flash of surprise brought his features back from the dead.

"I didn't give you much to go on," he said.

"Sure you did. You told me Root's a dead

end. Saved me time running down a bum lead."

"You believe me, then."

"You as much as told me you killed him, or was involved in his murder. In my eyes that writes your name in the golden book in the sky."

"I didn't —"

"Okay. You guessed. I didn't hire on to find out who killed him. The cops got manpower enough to chase that rabbit without my help. Frankly, I don't care. They know what they're signing on for when they take the oath."

"Py, see the man out."

The giant seemed to come awake then. He'd been sitting on some distant planet. As far as I could tell he'd forgotten what had passed between us, or for that matter who I was and where I'd come from. His problem appeared to go beyond a glandular aberration. I felt pity for him then. Being too big to buy your clothes in Walmart seemed challenge enough.

"Unnecessary," I said. "I left a trail of breadcrumbs from the front door."

"It's a slow day. You might get tackled on the way and lose your innocence. Half of Uncle's girls are slave labor, recruited from the street. You work up some muscle

Dumpster-diving for supper in Pyongyang."

He was being dramatic, a by-product of his former profession. On the way back through the Land of Cabbage I wasn't so sure. I couldn't see any faces, just eyes glowing back in the dimness between curtains in the doorways, like raccoons' watching the trash being put out.

With the prison town in my rearview mirror I had second thoughts, wondering why I hadn't asked Oakes Steadman about what George Hoyle had told me, about the seeming intimacy between Marcus Root and Paula Lawes. There was no reason to suspect a gang-banger would know everything that went on between a bent cop — if he was bent — and the public at large; then again, I wouldn't know without asking, even if he denied any knowledge of the situation. It was instinct on my part, pure and simple. The difference between Man and Beast is Beast doesn't question why it does what it does. There's something to be said for the inability to reason.

So what *did* I know, two busy days on the job? Everything the police did, provided they weren't holding something back, which of course they were, cops being cops the world over, plus the possibility that what had happened to Root just after he was first officer on the scene of Paula's disappearance had had nothing to do with that case. Everything Steadman had given me fit the blank space in the puzzle: the erratically driven Impala and the trajectory of the bullet that had killed him, suggesting it was fired from the low angle of a gang-driven hot rod. That being true, Paula's fate landed back in Francis X. Lawes's lap, right where John Alderdyce had said. But the piece popped right back up out of the puzzle when it came to why her murderer — if it *was* murder — would reopen the investigation because he had an uncontrollable urge to walk down the aisle. The insurance angle was too police-pat: No creditor was so impatient he couldn't wait a year for a piece of a million.

Was it simply a matter of someone who'd read too much of Ellery Queen and Agatha Christie, hoping to clear himself of suspicion by placing himself back in the spotlight of official scrutiny?

Nuts to that. He was a politician, even if he'd never run for office. Perception is reality. Clear in the eyes of evidence is clear. Only a masochist would do a 180 and willingly place himself back in the hot seat, like a horse running back into a blazing stable.

Anyway I had to believe that, if I intended to continue shaving in front of a mirror.

For the time being at least.

When old midnight came along this time I was still asleep, but just beneath the surface. I could hear myself snoring, and was beginning to be aware that I wasn't really standing on the deck of Captain Hook's ship in Jockey shorts and a cowboy hat; that old recurring dream that bore no resemblance to anything I'd been exposed to recently, and meant nothing to anyone but a therapist. Something tinkled in the kitchen, a clean crisp sound I wouldn't have heard if I'd been under any deeper. It was probably a spoon sliding into a bowl in the sink, a victim of gravity.

Just in case the spoon had eyes and sinister intent, I lifted the .38 from the nightstand, put on my street shoes, and headed that direction through coconut-milk moonlight. In shorts and oxfords I was no fashion plate, just a disappointment to anyone who wanted to stomp on my feet.

I crept along the living room wall and paused beside the square arch to the kitchen, breathing through my mouth and listening. A solitary cricket played the same two notes over and over, stopped when I stirred, waited, then when I didn't move again went back to the first bar and started over. The refrigerator thumped and purred. Apart from that nothing. I took in a lungful of air and swiveled around the edge of the arch, gripping the revolver against my hip and palming up the light switch on the wall.

I was alone with the cricket, the major appliances, and something that glittered on the table in the breakfast nook.

I left it there and checked the garage for unwanted guests. I was alone. The window was open. There was a fresh yellow scar where someone had pried loose the catch with a knife. Someone else had broken in that same way once, and although I'd refastened the screws I hadn't gotten around to replacing the rotted frame. This one, too, had picked the lock on the door to the kitchen. That used to be a semi-skilled process, but anyone with an Internet connection can download a tutorial. I hadn't bothered to install a dead bolt. I had nothing in the house worth the effort.

Until now.

Back in the kitchen I put down the .38 and picked up the foreign object. It was a ring. A diamond the size of a grape nested in an elaborate setting of white gold or platinum. I fetched my glasses to read what was etched inside the band: *Francis to Paula: Semper Votre.*

FIFTEEN

My go-to guy for evaluations and such didn't put up a glossy front on the ground floor of a downtown skyscraper, surrounded by glass cases and a plainclothes guard trying to look like an unobtrusive customer. His a/k/a this season was Harry Lauder; last time it was Ben Bernie, and Rod LaRoq the time before that. He always named himself after forgotten movie stars.

"Beats John Smith and Bob Jones," he said. "It's the next best thing to being invisible. Cops are getting younger all the time. Kids today got no interest in learning anything that happened thirty seconds before the miracle of their birth. By the time they catch on to Harry Lauder, I'm Vilma Banky."

"Vilma was a woman," I pointed out.

"So they waste their time looking for some dame."

Yeah, he talks like that; straight from the

132

bottom half of a double bill.

His given name is Eugene Orbit. At least that's the name on his one and only arrest report, for selling saxophones from a shipment that went missing in Sandusky, Ohio. The judge dismissed the case when the arresting officer failed to show up at the preliminary hearing, owing to incarceration for transmuting two kilos of heroin in the police property room into plaster of Paris.

Orbit's a bizarre-looking creature, assembled in a hurry from odd lots. His ears blossom out only a third of the way down from the top of his hairless head; his eyes are set far apart and stand out so far, some swore, he could swivel them independently like a chameleon. His beak hangs down in front of a tiny mouth, the bulbous tip quivering like a drop of water on the lip of a faucet. From there on down his face plunges into his frayed collar without pausing long enough to form a chin. He isn't tall, he isn't short, and as for his age he could pass for sixty or a hundred and six. I know from rumor that he's been fencing stolen merchandise all over the city since LBJ conducted affairs of state from the toilet.

The nearest thing he takes to a foolish risk is refusing to conduct business outside Detroit proper. The metropolitan area is such a sprawl he could squirrel himself up in any one of some forty-five independent communities, playing a constant shell game with the authorities and their separate jurisdictions, always a step outside their line. But he was born in a house Henry Ford himself had built for the workers in the River Rouge plant, is proud of his origins, and to my certain knowledge has never ventured north of Eight Mile Road or west of Telegraph.

This particular spring he'd set up shop in a one-story brick building with a flat asphalt roof on the cusp of Dearborn, with CORKY'S TV REPAIR scripted in green neon above the entrance. Steel utility shelves set up in stacks perpendicular to the walls contained dusty, obscenely naked picture tubes, amputated knobs, cartons of screws and washers, smaller tubes lying on their sides with tags attached to them like ancient scrolls, and an array of mystery components not quite as old as the Sphinx. A coffin-shaped walnut console minus its TV, radio, and turntable made a workbench behind the counter, with a metal Curtis Mathes chassis turned over on its side on top, its bundle of wires curled around it like the tail of a sleeping fox. There was a plain door leading to a back room where the real merchandise would be stored: Waterford crystal, giant flatscreens, maybe a set of Maserati rims, smoking hot.

"Kind of high-profile for you," I said, tilting my head toward some of the obsolete bric-a-brac. "These days a TV fix-it shop sticks out as far as Chapel Rock."

"Sometimes a yuppie living in one of them converted warehouses on the river drops in to keep the retro thing going in his apartment. If it's a busted plug, I fix it. If it's anything else I tell 'em I'm backed up to December; by which time I'll be in business someplace else. Apart from that nobody bothers me but the legits."

In Orbit-LaRoq-Bernie-Lauder's world, the crooks he deals with on the supply side are legits; everyone else is a chump. "Who's Corky?"

"Nobody, now. His widow threw in the sign with the lease. So far it's kept them spooks in that lunch wagon down the street from coming in here."

"Local cops?"

"Naw. Only the feds are dumb enough to peddle ham sandwiches in a Muslim neighborhood."

All the time we were speaking he was wrapping a square package the size of a toaster oven in brown paper and string from an old-fashioned dispensing spool bolted to the counter. It could be a vintage portable television, but I wouldn't lay odds on it. I lent him a finger while he tied the cord, then he slid the package aside and placed his palms flat on the countertop. That was my signal to finish the small talk and state my business.

I took a twist of tissue from a side coat pocket and opened it on the counter. The diamond caught cold fire in the light of the ceiling fluorescents, with a touch of green from the neon glowing outside the big plate-glass window.

He picked it up, hefted it on his palm. Then he screwed a jeweler's loupe into one of his distended eyes and turned the ring around in his fingers, examining it from all angles, including the inscription inside.

" 'Semper Votre,' what's that, French?"

"Latin. 'Always yours.' It sounds more poetic in the language of Rome." I met his naked eye. "You pick up some things in the craft."

"Nothing worth jackshit in this one. Who's Francis, the Pope?"

"Sinatra. Is it genuine?"

Keeping the loupe in place, he produced an eyedropper and a bottle of water from the shelf under the counter. He drew some water into the dropper, squeezed it onto the stone, and studied the effect through the lens. "Oh, it's the goods. Look how the drops puddle in the imperfections." He held out the loupe. I passed. Whatever was wrong with his eyes might be contagious.

"It's flawed?"

"All diamonds have flaws. That's how you know they're diamonds. I should charge you for these lessons." He put the loupe in his shirt pocket and used the tissue to wipe off the ring. "So when'd you decide to stop being a chump?"

"It's not for sale. I'm asking what it's worth."

"In that case, it's worth plenty. Carat and a half minimum, platinum setting worked by a true artist. I was going to offer a couple of thou, but you'd get twenty times that on the open market; more if you separate the stone from the ring and approach two different dealers. A lot of them that call theirselves honest try to Jew you down on engagement and wedding rings, on account of all the couples that split, flooding the market with returns. The crooks."

"It's worth forty grand?"

"Hang on." A jeweler's scale materialized from the shelf underneath. He put the ring on one of the pans and placed some coin-shaped weights in the other; played mix-

and-match with the weights. "Quarter over one and a half. Make it forty-five. Seriously, I can go thirty cents on the dollar if you give me a couple days to line up a buyer."

"I'll think about it." I rewrapped the ring and put it back in my pocket. "What's the damage?"

"You on an expense account?"

"If I were, would I tell you?"

"That means you are. Hundred, out the door."

"Spoken just like a TV repairman." I slipped him a century from Francis Lawes's stash. He scribbled on a receipt pad as old as the contents of the shop, signing it "Corky."

I stepped outside, turned up my collar against an icy snotty rain, and went back to my car, richer than I'd been in my life. I just didn't know what to do with the windfall. Not what the ring was worth: That belonged to Lawes, if he stood to inherit Paula's estate. As for what it meant in terms of useful information, so far as I knew I was still as poor as Job.

SIXTEEN

You could call the Lawes house a ranch style, but cheesy builders had been heaping offal on that term since Eisenhower. This one occupied some four thousand square feet on an oblong lot of close-shorn grass at the end of a paved cul-de-sac in Birmingham, which was no longer the community where the newly rich stopped for cocktails before stepping into old money in Grosse Pointe, where the Dodge brothers used to squirt their chaw into gold-plated spittoons. For decades now it's been the chief local employer of Micronesian gardeners, Guatemalan housekeepers, and chauffeurs named Fritz. The contractor had tricked out the brick exterior to make it look as if the courses had been laid by Rameses the Great and a carefully corroded tin likeness of the Greek goddess Diana aimed its bow-and-arrow toward Bloomfield Hills, the city's rival, from its rooftop perch. Four big windows with functional green shutters pierced the front wall on either side of a door with crystal panes in X-shaped leaded frames.

The doorbell disappointed, making an ordinary chiming noise when I pressed the button. After George Hoyle's Big Ben, anything else was bound to let me down.

Holly Pride answered it. Today it was a simple sleeveless top, powder-blue, charcoal slacks with a cutthroat crease, and blue strap sandals. Her bangs still slanted, but this time the rest of the outfit left my equilibrium intact.

"Small world," I said.

"You act surprised."

"I expected a bell-shaped woman named Constanza, with a moustache. You could bring down the neighborhood property values opening the door yourself."

"If you must know, I came to drop off some papers that needed signing. Francis took a personal day."

"Is he available?"

"He's resting upstairs. I know better than to disturb him when his bedroom door is closed."

"I don't. I need to see him."

"You found something?"

"Something found me."

A cheek got sucked, emphasizing the sharp line of the bone. "I'll never learn your language."

"You don't have to. You're not my client. Seriously, I need to talk with him before I can take another step." I had a hand in a flap pocket, Noël Coward style, fingering the diamond ring.

"You're forgetting I tried to pay you to take no steps at all."

"I remembered. Do I wait till he wakes up, then tell him you stopped me from conferring with him? Not a good move on the part of the eager bride-to-be."

"Oh, shit. Come in." She swiveled away, giving me room to pass.

We were in a cool dim living room, illuminated only by weak sunlight. A big fireplace built of the same prematurely aged brick as the outside supported a gray marble mantel, with squishy-looking silver-colored leather chairs arranged at angles facing the hearth and above the mantel a framed greatly enlarged print of a thistle. This matched the tattoo on Holly's ankle. She'd marked her territory.

To the left was a pony wall, beyond which a hallway led to the east end of the building. To the right, a paneled door painted gloss white stood open to a room with granite counters. That made it the kitchen; by the process of elimination, the hallway that ran left would lead to the master bedroom. I started that way.

"Wait," she said. "It's better if he hears my voice outside his door. Francis keeps guns. He was broken into once."

"I've got him beat." I made a gentlemanly gesture toward the hallway with my hand.

It was a broad passage, nearly wide enough to partition off into two small rooms, with the kind of art you usually see in houses like that on the walls: swirls of color that looked like oil on water, primary hues gridded into squares of varying sizes, a zombie wailing on a bridge, comic-strip panels blown up as big as king-size beds. Certain homeowners buy such things by the cubic foot.

The hall ended at another shiny white door. I stood aside while Holly rapped her knuckles on a panel. "Fran? It's me, sorry. Walker wants a sit-down."

Silence answered.

She went through it all again.

Again, nothing.

I felt a tingle I'd felt before. I'd learned a long time ago not to try to talk myself out of it.

She looked a question at me. I grasped

the knob. It turned without resistance. Closing my hand around the butt of the Chief's Special and flashing Holly a signal, I pressed the door gently with my palm and let it drift open on its own as we moved in two directions parallel to the walls on either side of the opening.

Nobody screamed. No shots rang out. A boulder didn't roll down a ramp, sending us scrambling for safety. The place was as silent as any can be in a world filled with automobiles, jet engines, dogs, children, and rolling boomboxes. Birmingham, at least, is wrapped in cotton wool, so that all that row was part of a soundtrack belonging to a different theater. We unpasted ourselves from the walls and I led the way inside, still gripping the .38.

No lights were burning, but the rheumy rays of the sun picked out a king-size bed with an upholstered bench at the foot, a highboy too tall to have been built in any recent century, a five-bladed fan suspended motionless from a high ceiling, and a pair of nightstands in a room large enough to accommodate three times as much furniture.

Francis Lawes lay atop the bedspread, fully dressed except for his feet in lisle socks, a white dress shirt tucked into his slacks with the collar open, no necktie. His legs were spread slightly and one arm hung over the left edge of the mattress. A bottle of Glenfiddich stood on the nightstand on that side and the sour essence of liquor smelled secondhand hung in the air. He should have been snoring, but the only breathing I heard belonged to Holly Pride and me. Maybe he hadn't drunk enough to soften his adenoids, or whatever it was that caused the roaring and spluttering of a sot at rest.

There was nothing for a detective in that. Times are stressful. We're all of us entitled to take off work now and then for a good toot, especially Scotch in the right bottle. I didn't see anything I disapproved of, except for the slender square semiautomatic pistol lying on the fawn-colored carpet below his dangling hand.

"Is that his gun?" I was whispering, God knows why.

"I wouldn't know." The words grated against her throat.

I stepped over and crouched over the weapon. It was a Glock 17L, the competition model with the extended barrel. It was too much gun for the room. I put my ear almost to the carpet — sculpted, with a pad

144

under it thick enough to withstand a season at Comerica Park. I might have been an Indian listening for an iron horse to come thundering up the tracks. I couldn't smell spent powder, but to do the thing right I'd have to pick up the pistol and stick the muzzle up my nose. Adding my prints to the mix wasn't an option.

I stood, creaking a little, folded my arms across my chest, and stared down at the still figure on the bed. Nothing brilliant of the old school of detecting suggested itself to me; but then why should it start now.

He lay as motionless as a rack of ribs.

Francis X. Lawes. He'd asked me to call him X. Maybe I should have. It didn't seem too much to grant a man during the last days of his life.

I unfolded my arms and reached down to grope for signs of activity in the big artery on the side of his neck. I didn't expect to find any, but I'm thorough, if not by any stretch of the imagination an optimist.

He shot up straight from the waist, eyes wide open, shouting, "What the hell!"

SEVENTEEN

When I climbed back down from the goddess Diana, Holly lay halfway across Lawes, hugging him around the shoulders and planting kisses all over his flushed face. Along with his exclamation, a gust of Highland heather — once removed — had come out, and what was left of it hung in the room like an old hammock. His mouth lay open where he'd left it and he was blinking a rapid Morse code. His eyes made their way around to me.

"Jesus, you scared the —"

"Welcome to my world. You looked like the front page of *The Police Gazette* when we came in. What's with the artillery?"

"The — ? Oh." He looked down at the gun on the carpet, patted Holly on the back, and disentangled himself. "I knocked it off the table reaching for the glass. I figured it could wait till I got up."

"Which wouldn't have been anytime soon.

146

If that bottle was full when you started, I'm running out and buying shares in Scottish grain futures. Any particular reason you decided to board the D.T. one-oh-nine?"

"English, please. Even that's too rich for my head." He spread a hand to grip both temples at once. That settled the question of his sobriety. The hangover only kicks in when you're drying out.

"Why the bender?"

"I spent all day yesterday trying to get a politician to stop acting as if the layout on a city contract is coming from his own pocket. I got through to him finally that a million saved is ten million earned in the campaign fund for his re-election if it means a hundred fewer potholes. Six hours and a dozen phone calls just for that. Yeah, I made the executive decision to stay home and drink myself into the Twilight Zone. Got a problem with that? Who let you in, anyway? Well?" he said when I let a second's silence pass.

"Just wondering which question you wanted me to answer. No to the first. As for the answer to the second, you're wearing her lipstick."

He took the hand from his forehead to mop his face; not that Holly's transparent gloss had left any tracks. A man who cared for his appearance as much as he did — when he wasn't sleeping one off — would straighten his necktie before grabbing a mortal wound.

"Holly?"

She was shrugging wrinkles out of her outfit. "He wanted to see you. I asked him if he found something. He said it found him. Whatever that means. If I knew you were —"

"Of course, darling." He put just enough sap into the response to make it fly. It was gone when he got back to me. "So?"

I looked at Holly. "Some strong coffee would help clear his head."

"I'm an office manager, not an intern. Why don't you make it yourself?"

"Because I need to talk to your boss-slash-fiancé alone."

Lawes said, "She can stay. We don't have any secrets."

"Bully for you. I do. I hate to trouble you," I told the woman in a different tone, "but coffee sure would go down good right now."

Strangely enough, that seemed to satisfy her. Another time it wouldn't. God made women, I didn't. She let herself out of the room, pulling the door to quietly behind her; not quite shut. I shrugged. What she heard didn't matter as long as she wasn't in the room. Conducting a face-to-face interview with an extra face present is like observing a wild animal in captivity; the results are inconclusive.

When I turned back toward the bed, the man in it had switched his body with X., confidant of civic leaders and millionaire contractors. The whites of his eyes were clear. His hair, rumpled from sleep, was as smooth as porcupine quills and he was sitting propped up against a pillow, shoulders squared, hands folded in his lap. He managed to make the space between us seem as substantial as an executive desk.

"You really thought I was dead? I'm beginning to doubt your talents as a detective."

"Talent's for trumpet players. This is a job. You hired me to prove your wife's dead. If you'd hired me to prove you weren't, I might have gone about it differently. Probably not, though. All that was missing was the organ music."

"Just what was it you found? Or that found you? If I spoke in meetings the way you do, I'd still be keeping books for Norway Cement in Westland."

"I'll let this do my talking for me." I drew out the twist of tissue and let it unwind itself so the ring tumbled out into his lap.

He looked at it a long moment before picking it up and turning it around, studying it from all sides, including the inscription inside the band. He returned it. "Is it supposed to mean something?"

"Whoever broke into my house and put it on my kitchen table thought so."

"It's been a long time. It *could* be the ring I gave her when we became engaged; the inscription is simple enough that I might have ordered it and forgotten. On the other hand, someone might have smuggled in a fake just to throw off your investigation."

"Okay." I rewrapped it and put it back in my pocket.

His dark brows almost touched his pale hairline. "No argument?"

"No." I turned toward the door, where the aroma of brewing coffee was creeping into the room.

"May I ask why?"

I turned back. "There's not much point in arguing with an accomplished liar. You've had too much practice haggling with politicians. I should have known that when I sent Holly out. I wanted to see your reaction without a third party in the room."

"So I'm a smooth-faced hypocrite? I can live with that. I've been called worse." He refolded his hands. "Just for the sake of discussion, why would I lie?"

"Because whoever put this in my house wants me to think the woman it belongs to is still above ground; either that, or he — or she — got it off her bony finger, or has been sitting on it all these years waiting for the opportunity to make something off it. If Paula's alive, you're still married, and this whole process will have to start all over again. I don't think that's what you want; so of course the ring isn't genuine according to you."

His face started to darken. I stopped him before he could open his mouth. "Don't bother. That would mean I don't think you killed her. There's no murderer without a victim."

"You thought I killed her?"

"The police do; but they've been on the case longer. I'm too new to it to start thinking. That comes later. So what I do now is back up, turn around, and look for proof she's alive instead of that she isn't. If that nullifies our agreement, I'll figure out how much I've spent from the retainer you gave me and we'll settle up."

The aroma grew stronger while he thought. Crockery clinked from the direction of the kitchen. "Keep at it," he said then. "Let me know what more you'll need to cover your time and expenses. If you produce a corpse or a living woman, it amounts to the same thing. At last I'll know the truth, and so will the police. If it turns out she's still among the living, at the very least it will take them off my back. The prospect of a divorce, however unpleasant, is preferable to this lingering suspicion."

"That's what everyone says." I didn't add that almost everything is worse than what you anticipated. A detective could lose work being frank. What I said was:

"All right. I'll press Reset and get back on the belt."

Holly nudged the door open and came in, carrying two cups and saucers and a steaming carafe on a tray. She stopped this side of the threshold. "Conference over? I can go back and make scones."

"Don't be cross, darling." Lawes caught my eye and pointed his chin toward the pocket where I'd slipped the ring. I took it out and handed it to her.

She did everything he had, then gave it back. "Is it hers?"

"That's the question for the bonus round," I said, turning the ring around and around in my fingers. I told her how it had come into my possession and what had passed between Lawes and me.

"Ridiculous! If she's alive, why wouldn't she show herself in person?"

I rolled a shoulder. "Lots of reasons. I can't think of any just now, but give me time."

"There's no giving about it. You're selling it to us, at the rate of five hundred a day."

"You've been talking," I told Lawes.

"There was no reason not to, now that she knows everything else."

She was watching him. She nodded toward the ring. "How could you not recognize it?"

"I'm a man. As soon as we throw money at a thing we forget about it. It's only a symbol after all."

She scowled. "About fifty thousand dollars' worth of symbol."

She had a head for figures.

"Forty-five," I said. "It has flaws."

"All diamonds have flaws."

"Women are born knowing such things. Jewelers and fences have to learn it. Detectives too." I chewed a cheek. There didn't seem to be anything to lose, so I asked Lawes the question. "Did Paula ever mention a cop named Marcus Root?"

He looked puzzled. He was human after all. The hangover had suggested it, but here was proof. "No. Who's he?"

"Was. He was the first cop on the scene

where Paula's car turned up without her in it. You must have heard the name when the cops talked to you."

"Maybe. I don't remember. I had a bit more on my mind."

"He was killed that same night. It was on the news."

"Again —" He shrugged. "But why should she have mentioned him at all? She vanished before he came on board."

I gnawed on the other cheek. I said, "No reason," and let myself out.

It wasn't the time to bring up George Hoyle. A promise is a promise. Until it isn't.

It took me four blocks to spot it; an embarrassment. Back when I had a partner to take up the slack, the vehicular tail was one of my specialties. I could paste myself to a subject's rear bumper for miles without tipping my hand, and when *I* was the subject, I nailed the shadow straightaway. But working alone for so many years had dulled the fine edge.

There was, of course, a question of profile. The rearview gave me nothing, but when I turned a corner I caught it in the side mirror. That mirror was set at a slightly different angle, just enough to catch a vehicle hugging the pavement almost at curb level.

Gang low-riders are like Stealth bombers, sliding literally below the radar.

EIGHTEEN

In that situation there are three choices to be made. It's always three, and always the same. I could lose the tail, confront it, or string along with it until I knew who was behind it and why.

The list is in ascending order of risk. You might think turning around and bracing the party is the most dangerous, but if you do it right and keep surprise on your side, you cut the hazard in half. Ducking it is the easiest, in a town I know as well as the face I shave, where the cops let you drive as fancy as you like so long as you don't wreck the bell curve, and with my track record in that area of enterprise. But playing dumb and just carrying on is like zip-lining through a tiger pit; you give your pursuer space to arrange a plan of battle, with no clue as to how good he is at it. The longer you maintain slack, the better his chances and the worse yours. It's all a matter of timing, same

156

as diving off the Great Barrier Reef and microwaving popcorn.

Leaving this one in the dust was the course to take, no doubt about it; doing a 180 and bearding him in the act was next best. So of course I did nothing, taking him on the scenic tour, on the off-chance he'd tip his hand before giving me the same deal as Officer Marcus Root.

He was good; that much I established in the first five minutes. Drawing him around Grand Circus Park at the base of Woodward, I spotted him only once, when he gunned his motor to avoid losing me on the first curve; the combination of after-market horsepower and glass-pack exhaust system soared above the monotonous hum of lesser engines like a panther's cry in a teeming jungle. After that it was mostly guesswork: a seeming empty space between trailing cars in bumper-to-bumper circumstances, a javelin-shaped reflection sliding across the ground-floor windows of the Book Cadillac Hotel on Michigan, a prickling at the back of my neck when there'd been no concrete evidence for a dozen blocks.

He was as good as his machine, not some green initiate set on me to prove himself worthy of the colors. That was enough information for now. From Monroe, I feinted a left onto Randolph, a one-way street, and when I calculated he'd taken the bait I spun around and took off against the flow of traffic. Horns flattened the air, a siren whooped; but by then I was on Lafayette, obeying all the signs with a solid wall of traffic between me, the cops, and Lowboy.

My shoulders were tented up around my ears. Willing myself to relax, I shifted positions. The ring in my side pocket poked a dent in my hip.

That made up my mind. I swung back toward the river and entered the lot next to the Reliance building and inserted my heap between a pair of vehicles so nondescript they stood out like circus wagons. I was halfway to the front door when I turned back, unshipped the .38 in its clip from my belt, and locked it in the glove compartment. The place had more metal detectors than Detroit Metropolitan Airport and the people who monitored them were a lot less cordial than the TSA.

Four-ten was open this time. John Alderdyce sat at the pale-blue metal desk, scribbling with a ballpoint pen. Today was casual, at least from the waist up: burgundy cashmere shirt buttoned to the neck, emphasizing the deep purplish hue of the skin.

I tapped on the door. "Still doodling?"

"Totting up how many employees of this razor-sharp institution are duplicating each other's work. Ernest Krell's spinning in his Frigidaire."

The prevailing wisdom — if it ever prevailed anywhere — was that according to the terms of his will, the founder of Reliance Security Services had been cryogenically preserved in a facility in upstate New York, until such time as a cure could be found for terminal arrogance. "Who made you the presiding efficiency expert?"

"It's this or crossword puzzles, which drive me nuts. I can't convince *The New York Times* there's no such thing as a wild ox, unless they trot out the guy whose job is to strike off into the bush and castrate a feral bull." He folded his gold-rimmed glasses and tapped them on the desk. "Tell me you're here to announce Francis Lawes's arrest."

I shook my head. "My previous record stands." I laid the ring on the sheet he'd been writing on and spread the tissue.

He looked at it as if a fly had landed there. Then he put the glasses back on his nose and picked it up. He went straight to the engraved inscription.

"He give it to you?"

"No." I told him how I got it.

"He identify it?"

"No again. But if what he hired me to do is what he hired me to do, denying it makes sense."

"Because he'd have to free himself the hard way, through the courts."

"If that's what he wants. If he killed her, I still don't see why he'd want to pay me to stir up the same old dust."

He placed it back in the center of the crumple. "What makes it my business?"

"I want to find out where it came from, what jeweler, and who he sold it to. If it was Lawes, then I'll know it's a clue and I can concentrate on who delivered it to my place. If it isn't, I'll know that some third party is trying to roil the waters."

"So take it to Deb Stonesmith. She's got the resources."

"Also a public blotter. I need someone who still has contacts but doesn't have to go on record. I peddle discretion; it's the most popular product in my inventory. Once the newsbirds find out that the story's grown a new set of legs, they'll trample all over the footprints and lost buttons I need to piece together the puzzle and unveil the answer. Preferably during a formal dinner party with all the suspects in attendance."

"What's in it for me?"

"Your per diem, to keep it strictly on the up-and-up with the brass here. Mainly your own peace of mind: Lawes in custody, or Lawes cleared of suspicion. Don't try to tell me it hasn't been working on you all this time."

"Like a flesh-eating virus."

Him and Commander Albert White. I don't know what it is about cops. They can't wait to get in their thirty and skedaddle. Then they spend another thirty chewing over the gristle they left behind.

Someone rapped on the open door. "John?"

Alderdyce aimed a scowl past my shoulder. I shifted my weight and looked at a middle-aged party in a white short-sleeve dress shirt, black necktie, and a belly hanging over the waistband of his tan Dockers. He wore his hair in bangs, Three Stooges style. A goose bump of a nose was marooned in the middle of his big pink face. White-painted pencils stuck out of a plastic sleeve in his breast pocket like pickets in a fence. He'd shipped here straight from Cape Canaveral, 1961.

"Dale." The man behind the desk turned a palm my way. "Dale Grange, Amos Walker. Dale manages the joint."

Eyes like white grapes took me in. "Are you a client of this firm?"

"A colleague." I dealt him a business card. "Ernest Krell used to farm out some work my way. I'm hoping to return the favor."

He held the card by one corner, as if a rat dangled from it. "Reliance is in the domestic defense business. We haven't worked with independent operators in years."

Alderdyce's face went flat. "I've known Walker most of my life. A little professional courtesy goes a long way."

"With Krell, maybe. That marble head you pass in the lobby every day is all that's left under this roof." He stuck the card back at me.

"Keep it. I got it on a twofer."

Dale Grange looked at his watch. He wore it strapped to the underside of his wrist. That settled his account as far as I was concerned. People who wear it that way like to sneak looks when you're boring them. "At Reliance, we measure time in microseconds. We've already wasted a couple of hundred of them discussing this. Thank you for dropping in, Mr. —"

"Hawkshaw," I said. "I guess you were too busy counting microseconds to listen when we were introduced."

Alderdyce rewound the ring in tissue and

put it in a cashmere pocket. "I'll get back to you with what I find out."

The white grapes swam back his way. "Mr. Alderdyce, if you don't like the way we do things around here —"

"I don't." When he rose to his feet, it was always an event, like Gibraltar shrugging its shoulders.

"In that case, pack your things."

He stooped and lifted a stout cardboard carton from inside the kneehole of the desk. "I never unpacked."

"God, that felt good."

We were riding down in the elevator. I asked if a favor for a friend was worth losing his job.

"Since when are we friends?"

"Since the last time you tanked me for obstruction of justice. You could have had me broken in Lansing, but you forgot. You never forget anything."

"That's one of the things I regret not forgetting."

"Not an answer to my question."

He toggled his big head on his big neck, cracking bones. "I lost a shot at chief of detectives and twice the amount of my current pension for worse reasons. I've been looking for an excuse to tell that son of a bitch to screw himself since the day I signed on. What have you dug up, besides an ugly piece of expensive jewelry?"

I filled him in on what White and Oakes Steadman had said about Marcus Root.

He remembered the case. "I know Steadman. We worked with Allen Park on a protection racket the gangs were working both sides of the line. I wouldn't trust him as far as the end of my arm. Probably why the staties recruited him. You can expect a crook to be untrustworthy. Legits are a crapshoot."

"What about White?"

"Fellow cop. Also a crapshoot. What else?"

"Paula Lawes may have known Root."

"Based on what?"

"Don't crowd me, John."

The doors opened. We walked through the drafty lobby. Ernest Krell paid us no attention from his pedestal.

Out in the parking lot, Alderdyce unlocked his car by remote. It was a silver Mazda, that year's model. He dumped the box into the backseat, scraped nonexistent dust off his palms, and faced me. "What happened to 'I don't have to scribble on a blotter'?"

"Not the same deal. This was a personal promise, in return for information. I'll throw some expense money your way."

"Not if it's Lawes's."

"If this clears him, it won't bend your almighty principles."

"Maybe not, but it'd chafe my ass. I've spent too much time not liking him to change my tastes."

I shook out a cigarette and speared it in the corner of my mouth. I didn't light it. Cigarettes are good for many other things besides destroying your lungs. "Then I'll put it on my account."

He laughed. You don't want to hear John Alderdyce laugh. "You couldn't cover my gas. Anything else?"

I thought about the low-rider I'd dusted off my tail. There was no sign of it in the lot or the street that ran past it. I hadn't expected one, but I'd been wrong before when I thought I was in the clear.

I said nothing. I didn't know why, except that it was my headache. He had enough on his mind, beginning with filing for unemployment.

NINETEEN

Our most bipolar season was running true to form. Sunshine skulked in at an oblique angle, hoping not to attract the attention of a solid shelf of indigo overcast hanging low above it. The light in those circumstances is Turneresque, an angry mix of orange and green, pregnant with foreboding.

I didn't feel any of that. With my only solid lead out of my hands, I stood before a blank wall that offered no handholds to hoist myself over it. At such times I run to ground to drink, smoke, and think. Rosecranz was in the middle of his quadrennial spring cleaning, heaving open windows in the vacant offices to change out the stale air for the variety that came from the street, pushing dust bunnies, dead skin cells, fly husks, and stained cotton swabs out into the halls with a long-handled broom, and touching up the wainscoting with a fresh application of dollar store shellac over a generation of dirt. The building reeked of Pine-Sol and forgotten tenants. I stepped over a pile of sweepings, collected my mail from under the slot, and sorted through it on the way to the desk. A coupon promising 50 percent off a jar of pickles at Sam's Club was the only piece that made it past the wastebasket.

The super hadn't opened my window, the office being under current lease and the door locked. I cracked it to expel the stench of World War II disinfectant, poured a glass from the bottle in the safe, lit a cigarette, and sat back to decipher the hieroglyphs in my notebook. But both the liquor and the cigarette tasted like turpentine, so I continued the work without benefit of refreshment.

Andrea Dawson was the other client still with Baylor, Schneider, Baylor, and Baylor who'd worked with Paula Lawes at the time she dropped off the grid. She was away in California when I'd called last time, but had been expected back the next day. I dragged over the phone and dialed the PR firm's number. My luck was good for once. I reached the cooperative soul who'd been so eager to help the first time, and he hadn't changed his mind.

The number he gave me belonged to a pharmaceutical lab operating out of a professional building in Southfield, with a menu as long as the Bayeux Tapestry. I entered Dawson's extension and got a voice I'd have called flinty if not for a faint dialect that stretched one-syllable words to two. The South had risen yet again. Most of the flint flaked off when I introduced myself and told her what I was working on.

"Ye-es, I remember Paula well. I'm not sur-ah what I can say that will help after all this ty-um." I'm breaking the spelling rules just once to establish the flavor of the magnolia marinade.

"That's what all the polite people say, Ms. Dawson."

"Miss, please. I dislike the smell of burning bras."

"Miss. May I ask what you do for your company?"

"I translate scientific shoptalk into plain English. Whenever we deliver a breakthrough in medical treatment, I stand behind a lectern and tell the boys and girls of the press what we've found in terms they don't have to look up in the Merck Manual. To put it bluntly, my bosses think I cut a better figure in front of a camera than some frump in a lab coat."

"So you're a spokesmodel."

"That doesn't offend me. When a serious

public-image issue rears its ugly head, some of these muckrakers choose not to hurl embarrassing questions at a pretty face. But don't think I didn't serve my time in the trenches first."

"That happens? The embarrassing questions, I mean."

A moment got milked. "This is all off the record, isn't it, sugar?"

"When you put it that way, how can I refuse?"

"As I said," she purred. "Let's just say that when the Food and Drug Administration overlooks a fatal side effect and clears a medication for distribution, it's we who sell it who take the hit. Who was it said a government bureau is the nearest thing to eternal life?"

"Ronald Reagan. Let's talk about Paula. How well did you know her?"

"We're like sisters. No, I'll amend that. Sis and I get along like two cats in a gunnysack. Paula's an only child, and with Belinda trying so hard to be a bee-eye-tee-see-aitch, we just naturally drifted into each other. If she had secrets I didn't know about, she'd forgot 'em."

My heart sped up a little, but I let that one steep. "Why so candid? We just met, and we haven't even done that, really."

169

Silver bells — tarnished a little and scratchy — rang back in her throat. That would be Viagra to most of the male population. "You can trust everybody or trust nobody, and get in the same trouble either way. Why not enjoy the company?"

"Who said that?"

"My daddy. When you needed chicken manure and lots of it, he was the man to see in North Carolina."

I believed that.

"Did Paula ever mention George Hoyle?"

"Oh, the record man." The molasses had gone clean out of her accent. "Well, it was discs back then. I don't know what it is now. Maybe he shoots *Little Black Sambo* straight into people's brains."

"For shame, Andrea. New South and all."

"I'm not Robert E. Lee, sugar. I kept my sword."

"You're not a fan of Hoyle's."

"You could say that. You could say if a gator swallowed him whole, I'd treat the gator to a free sample of our new gastric gummy."

"You know him, then."

"Never met him. Never care to. He got his fill of her favors, then dumped her over dessert in some hole-in-the-wall no self-respecting cockroach'd be found dead in."

"Was it the Gamesman Inn?"

"Maybe. Someplace you can't see your hand in front of your face — or the lady from next door nuzzling the mailman's neck. It was in Allen Park, that much I remember."

"Why'd he dump her?"

"He never said, according to Paula. She sobbed into my blouse all the rest of that night. Said she felt doubly damned on account of she was stepping out on her husband and had no right to carry on so. I said the one thing hadn't any to do with the other. A snake's a snake and it don't matter where the mouse came from or why. Then I poured her another glass of Southern Comfort."

"During all this confessing, did the name Marcus Root come up?"

Computer keys rattled on her end. I didn't think she was looking at the name, just killing time while she accessed her own memory. She was a multi-tasker. "Marcus Root. No."

"He was a police officer in Allen Park, if that helps."

"It sure does! She said a policeman she knew slightly dropped by their table that night. It was after he left that Hoyle's mood changed. I asked her if she thought the two things had anything to do with each other. She thought about it, then said no. I can't tell you if she believed what she said. When someone's in that state I doubt anyone could."

Something clanked, startling me. It was the steel rule I kept on the desk. I'd been standing it on end with my free hand, sliding my fingers down it, reversing ends, and starting again. I laid it aside. "Is there anything else about that night you remember?"

"Just that I was mighty glad when she went into the bathroom to freshen up and left. It must have been about three A.M. and I was exhausted. She hugged me at the door. That was the last time I saw her. I got busy not discussing a class-action lawsuit against the firm and I didn't hear from her, so I assumed she'd flung herself into her work. She was helping elect a governor at the time, which I suppose made a welcome distraction." She paused. The rattling had stopped. "Should I call you if I remember anything else? Or even if I don't?"

That last question came with an extra ladle of mint julep.

I grinned at the door to my waiting room. "Now, Miss Dawson. I could be a serial killer for all you know."

"A better-looking axe murderer I never heard tell of. I'm looking at your picture right now. The *Free Press* puts all its local morgue photos online. Did you really shoot that nasty hit man outside your office last year?"

"Oh, that picture. They dredged it up from the base of the Aswan Dam. It was taken ten years ago. I've put on a couple of pounds since then and gone grayer than a goose."

"This old gal don't mind a little snow on the roof."

I said I'd keep her number and rang off before she brought up my rap sheet.

My fingers drummed the receiver in its cradle. Sometime during the conversation, an imp had blown moist warm air in my ear. Whatever significance it carried had vanished along with the sensation. All I knew about it with any certainty was that it had been important.

I checked voice mail, in case Alderdyce had called with information on the ring I'd left with him. Nothing. Same with the cell. It was early yet.

My notebook opened to George Hoyle's number. That was a sign of some kind. I dialed it. I was working from the playbook some distant ancestor of Alderdyce's had assembled back when Caesar was dividing up Gaul like a personal-pan pizza. I'd been Dr. Jekyll the first time. After what I'd gotten from Andrea Dawson I was ready to dust off Mr. Hyde.

No answer. I looked at my watch. I had time for a late lunch, somewhere on the way to Harper Woods and Hoyle's medieval house.

My belly wasn't ready for food. Too much nicotine and too little useful information had irritated the lining.

I remembered my drink then. It had gone flat. The tank wash I could afford resumed the aging process as soon as it left the bottle, and not to the good. I got up, dumped the glass into the sink in the water closet, half-filled it from the tap, and drank from it as I walked to the window and looked out at the weather. Under it, a car I recognized idled close to the curb, smoke stuttering from its gleaming tailpipe. If it rode any lower it could have struck sparks off its bumper.

TWENTY

For a generation I'd parked on the lot belonging to the one-story building across the street from the office, a glazed-brick relic that had by turns sheltered a garage, a music shop, a distributor of medical marijuana, a dollar store, and a string of Mexican, Italian, Indian, Thai, and Vietnamese restaurants, each one as successful as the United Nations; but the scrap rats had finished the place for good. When they were through harvesting the copper wire and plumbing, they'd taken the hardware off the doors, pried the rebar out of the concrete slab, and severed the iron posts that supported the roof; all but one. They sawed halfway through it when the north end of the building fell in. The mortuary that got the city contract buried the pair in Mt. Elliott Cemetery in manila envelopes.

The half that remained standing was condemned, to await demolition at the end of the line of HUD hovels, crack houses, smash-and-grab ruins, and chain bookstores already selected to join the pattern of vacant lots that have turned Detroit into a jack-o'-lantern when seen from the air. The site, grandfathered in before local building codes prohibited construction on lots smaller than an acre, wasn't likely to attract visionary entrepreneurs, so that would continue to be the situation for the foreseeable future. There was no room to leave a car that wouldn't wind up under a pile of rubble come the first stiff wind from Canada, so I'd made arrangements to store the Cutlass in a patch of gravel behind a microbrewery three blocks down Grand River Avenue.

Low-Rider didn't know that, apparently; which was why he was waiting at the curb to see which way I turned after leaving my building.

It was one of the new Dodge Chargers, chopped and retro-fitted until it bore as much resemblance to a Chrysler product as a crocodile did to a French poodle. It was painted matte black, a finish that gave off no reflection, would be nearly invisible in darkness, and even in broad daylight could be overlooked if you were thinking about anything else while you were staring directly at it. Say what you like about paranoia, it has certain advantages.

I sipped water and thought. I'd already explored two of my options, stringing the tail along until I knew more about it and shaking loose of it in traffic. The hour had come to brace it.

Not head-on, though. If there's one thing age teaches a man, it's to avoid a frontal assault given other options.

Of all the code violations Rosecranz collected like phony green cards, the one requiring fire exits to remain accessible was what most concerned me at present. The door leading to the alley behind my building had been chained and padlocked since before Japan switched from plastic toys to automobiles. There was the fire escape on my floor, but I'd burned through my luck there once before; it's finite, after all. Just thinking about it set all my warning buzzers into action.

So it came down to a frontal attack after all. A man could save himself a lot of time just by embracing the most unpleasant plan at the start.

Uber wouldn't do, even if I landed a driver who wasn't a psycho; not conspicuous enough. What I needed was flash — so bright it could be seen from the space station, or at least a gang-banger driving a speed-bump on wheels.

Hollywood Limo ran a quarter-page display ad in the metropolitan directory, with the silhouette of a Rolls-Royce Silver Ghost, the slogan "Highway to the Stars," and a phone number that read TOP GLAM. It would be an enterprise established back when the state capital was peddling sweetheart tax deals to the motion picture industry to shoot movies in our state. Since that idea had been shot down by legislators, the business would be hanging on by its eyelashes with Chapter 11 snapping at its heels.

I called. I doubted I'd get the parade float pictured in the ad, but if the size of the notice meant anything, the place would be working hard to keep up appearances. In that neighborhood, even a modest town car with a vanity plate would draw lightning like a golfer with a tin hat.

"Hollywood Limo, you're the star."

I almost thumped the receiver on the desk to clear it of static. The voice sounded like an amateur impressionist imitating a professional imitating Cary Grant.

I gave him my name and location. Cary said, "Ten minutes, old sport."

Killing time, I counted the cash I had left from Lawes's advance. It was enough to get me to the end of the street with a decent tip to spare. That was farther than I needed to go, but someone has to encourage local business.

Just before leaving I got something else out of the safe: a Ruger Blackhawk with a dull finish and black Neoprene grips, checked the load, and traded it for the .38 on my belt. It was more gun than I liked, but street toughs like the one dogging me might take their chances with a garden-variety revolver; with a magnum, not so much.

Rosecranz had found a channel that broadcast Greco-Roman wrestling. In the foyer I could hear the grunts and the Slavic announcer's jabber from his office down the hall. The small window in the entry door gave me a view of the street directly in front of the building. I couldn't see the low-rider, but I knew it was there.

My ride squished to a stop just as I was crushing a butt on the linoleum. The car was better than I'd hoped, a late-model stretch Lincoln, amethyst-colored, with whip antennas and windows tinted as dark as the glass in an oven door. The wheel covers were polished to a mirror finish, with the silhouette of an old-fashioned Mickey Mouse–ear movie camera embossed in the centers, set independently of the rims so that the image was always right-side up. It wasn't as gaudy as the *QE II* nor as unobtrusive as the Ritz-Carlton Hotel. I strode across the sidewalk, looking up and down the street like Danny Kaye in a spy spoof, and let myself into the rear salon, pulling the door shut behind me with a crisp satisfying snick. Tufted leather enveloped me like bubble wrap. The interior smelled like an expensive luggage shop. It was almost suffocating.

A gleaming onyx face under a patent-leather visor hung over the back of the front seat. Out of its high-beam grin came a Jamaican accent. "Thirsty, mister? Plenty of the premium stuff back there in the bar."

Purely out of curiosity I lowered a hatch set into the back of the seat. The labels were as advertised, but they looked a little road-weary around the edges. "Dewar's in a pinch bottle I can overlook," I said. "If it's Old Smuggler, I'll put up a kick."

The grin dropped like a checkered flag. "I don't stock it, mister. Where to?"

I glanced at the side-view mirror mounted outside the front passenger's window. The top of a sleek roof showed just above the bottom edge. I folded a twenty and passed it across the seat. "Left lane. Take it slow up to Washington, then go as fast and as far as you want. I won't be here to tell on you."

"Where you want me to stop?"

"Time it so you're caught at the light."

"That where you're getting out?"

"No, I'll be gone by then. Just don't change course or look back when I jump out."

"Our insurance won't cover that!"

"No company in the world would. Don't worry, my estate can't afford a lawyer."

"Listen, if you're trying to lose somebody, you picked the right man. I got Lee Iacocca away from the press when he got Congress to bail him out; in a fucking Le-Baron yet."

"I'm not trying to lose anybody. Just the opposite. Drive, Andretti." I slid over to his side of the car.

But Andretti didn't drive. He stuck my twenty, still folded, back across the seat. "I've got a perfect record, boss." He cocked a shoulder, showing a five-year patch stitched on the sleeve. "I'm not shit-canning it for a double sawbuck."

I'd stashed a fifty in my right sock for emergencies; I'd almost forgotten it, which was the point. I dug it out and pushed it between the two fingers that held the twenty. His tongue bulged his cheek for several seconds. Then he reversed the hand, fisted the bills, and turned back around to grip the wheel.

Traffic was thin that time of day. It was a one-way street, giving him the opportunity to hug the curb that ran in front of the Bloody Run Brewery. The redbrick building bore a distressed metal sign showing a grinning Chief Pontiac scalping a chesty pioneer woman in gingham; Detroit is the last stand for the politically incorrect. I slid into a crouch, grasping the door handle and bracing for the leap.

The name on the chauffeur's license displayed for the benefit of his passengers was Jean-Claude Philippe, but the old grin showed in the rearview mirror, so I called him Smiley to myself. Driving prom-goers at the pace of a hearse doesn't offer much in the way of challenges. Anyway he came through as directed. He drove steadily at about ten miles per hour, forcing the bottom-scraping Dodge to creep along a full block behind. I glanced through the rear window just once — there was no point in looking again — and wriggled my hips to keep them from locking up.

One of the gaggle of temporary administrators who'd taken the place of our incarcerated mayor had spearheaded a drive to beautify the city with tree plantings, conveniently located in front of eyesores that the budget wouldn't stretch far enough to demolish. A full-press renovation on the part of Bloody Run's partners had rescued its quarters from condemnation in the interim, but the cottonwood on the corner hadn't been pruned since young adulthood; its branches, weighted down by fat, pubis-shaped leaves, screened most of the front entrance from the street. I waited until we passed the tree, then popped the door handle and threw the door open with all my weight. The cold mist felt good on my face; I was sweating in spite of the temperature. My bum leg reminded me why as I used it to push myself out into empty space.

I landed on my feet; in a manner of speaking. I made contact long enough to feel the earth through my soles, then obeyed a law of nature, tumbling forward, belly-bumping rock-hard ground, executing an Olympic-quality somersault, and scraping fabric and flesh off a shoulder when I lighted on my back against concrete fencing a window well belonging to the brewery's basement.

Tempting as it was, I didn't stay there waiting for my lungs to reinflate. I was up again before inertia overtook momentum, running around behind the building where my Cutlass stood on what was left of a paved parking lot belonging to the type-writer repair shop that had once occupied the building. I had the door open and myself behind the wheel before my leg remembered to start throbbing.

The engine — which is where I spend all the money I save on bodywork — caught with a bellow. I slammed the transmission into gear and spat gravel and chunks of asphalt off the rear tires, slewing right and left as I tore around the building toward the street.

When it comes to automobile ownership, there are certain advantages to maintaining a chalky finish, some surface rust, and more dings and dents than a linebacker's skull. I nudged shopping baskets out of parking spaces without a second thought, enjoyed ample room in my slot courtesy of more cautious motorists parked on both sides, and found uses for my machine other than simple transportation; two tons of Detroit steel make a fearsome projectile. The character in the Charger, on the other hand, had put half my year's pay into his paint job alone. Like having a child, such attention to appearances tends to rearrange one's perspective when it comes to dealing with jeopardy.

Also, there was a better-than-even chance

this one had made these investments at the cost of bothering to insure his vehicle against collision.

Smiley had missed the green light, as directed; a rare talent. The signal had changed again, and he was rolling across the intersection just above idle when I left the lot doing forty, scraping sparks off my undercarriage against the curb, pasted the foot-feed to the floor, and aimed straight at the gang-banger inching along behind the limousine.

The tree had provided the cover I'd hoped for. He was so intent on the car in front of him, thinking I was still a passenger, that he paid no attention to what was coming at him from left field until the wail of the big 455 under my hood made him turn his face toward the window on his side. At the speed I was approaching the face was only a pale oval with a black hole in it, wide enough to release whatever blasphemies sprang to mind in the instant. Almost too late he spun the wheel right and tromped on the pedal, scraping the rear bumper of the limo on the right with his left front fender just close enough to bruise the top layer of paint on the Charger. At the same moment I stood on my brakes with both feet. My tires howled, leaving twin strips of black on the pavement that will still be there come the invasion. The car traveling behind the hot rod, a Ford Flex shaped like a box of animal crackers, stopped just short of hitting me broadside. As I bronco-rode my shocks and springs, the Charger bucked up over the berm on the side of the street opposite the brewery, carved furrows in the damp grass on the corner, creased its twin pipes on the curb alongside Washington, swung left into that street, and huddled itself against the curb; as sweet a job of parallel parking as I'd seen.

There was a vacuum, as after a detonation. The pressure hurt my ears. The silence broke only when the driver of the Flex remembered to pat his horn and continued on his way. A whistling sound startled me; it was me breathing. I slammed the cane into reverse and backed up onto the lot belonging to Bloody Run. A scrum of customers and the owner, a Chaldean named Fakim, had gathered in front of the building to see the show. I killed the engine, pried my fists off the wheel, and opened my door to fall out.

■ ■ ■ ■

III
FORGETTING TO
REMEMBER

■ ■ ■ ■

TWENTY-ONE

The Charger was still parked on the wrong side of Washington, engine rumbling, the driver gripping the wheel with both hands. He was staring through the windshield and didn't seem to notice my approach. On the way I reached back for the Ruger and pawed at an empty holster. I'd lost the thing leaping out of the limo.

I'd come too far not to see it out. Turning away from the crowd across the street, I stuck a hand in my side pocket and tapped the window frame on the driver's side with my stiff forefinger.

That one was older than Castle Rock, but it worked. He jumped high enough to thump the headliner with the crown of his skull, turned toward me full-face, and lifted his hands from the wheel, showing me his palms.

He was a light-complexioned black with his hair buzzed to a reddish haze and features that looked as if they'd been applied against a fierce headwind: Eyes, nostrils, lips, and cheeks canted backward from the center of his face. He bore a close resemblance to the lead singer of Fine Young Cannibals.

Not that he'd be old enough to understand the reference. You know you're over the hill when the crooks and cops start looking like the kids on *Sesame Street.*

His window was open; as far as I could tell there was no glass on either side. His hands were still raised. I reached in, turned off the motor, and jerked the key from the ignition. I frisked him to the waist and ran my palm inside both his thighs, then groped at the door pocket. Finally I reached up to tip down the sun visor. If there was a gun in the car — and there would be — it wasn't within easy reach from the driver's seat. I backed up a step, gesturing with the hand in my pocket. "Unlock."

"Can't. Doors are welded shut."

I looked down. Sure enough, there was no outside handle. That explained the window situation. The car was built to race.

I walked around to the passenger's side, grasped the roof with both hands, chinned myself, and swung my legs through the opening. I landed on the bucket seat without grunting any more than a moose with a hernia and popped open the glove compartment. A Sig Nine lay on the manual that had come with the car. I worked the slide, kicking out the cartridge that was already in the chamber, said, "Tsk-tsk," and rested it on my lap with the muzzle pointing his way.

"Oakes told me never trust another man's gun. It might be missing the firing pin." He had a shallow voice with a street accent. It wobbled a little.

I went on looking at him, not down at the piece. "Nice try. That one's even older than sticking up a guy with a hangnail." I reached across with my other hand and patted the empty pocket.

"Aw, shit."

I grinned.

Somewhere in Detroit a siren gulped at an intersection.

"City's making a comeback," I said. "People are bothering to call the police." I handed him his key.

He looked down at it as if I'd tipped him a quarter.

"That means go, genius. If you're street legal, I'm Princess Kate."

He inserted the key and tickled the engine into life. The rumble made the soles of my feet tingle. Rubber chirped and we swung right on Grand River. He drove with both hands on the wheel. Hieroglyphic tattoos began on the backs of his hands, climbed inside the rolled-back cuffs of a denim jacket faded from blue to white, and erupted from his scoop collar, scaling his neck almost to his chin.

At Madison Avenue I directed him to turn right and drew my finger across my throat as we came abreast of a gray stone pile that looked like a mausoleum. He slid alongside the curb and drew the emergency brake. "What's this?"

"Music hall. It's the least likely place to draw cops. Oakes Steadman sent you?"

"I didn't say that."

I swatted his ear with the barrel of the Sig. He howled, clapped a hand to the ear, and drew it away to inspect it for blood. "You busted my eardrum!"

"Don't exaggerate. In a day or two the ringing will stop. You introduced Steadman into the conversation, I didn't. What's he afraid of?"

"He ain't —" He cut himself off, seeing me lift the gun again from my lap.

I lowered it. "I parted friends with him and his golem, I thought. What's he up to, sending you after me with a street cannon?"

"He didn't," he said, shielding his ear with

his palm. "He said to keep an eye on you, make sure you don't draw any fire."

"Fire from who?"

" 'My past associates.' What he said."

"His old gang? What am I to them?"

"Just somebody that might've been seen meeting him. Not all of Oakes's old friends are happy he's snuggling up with the cops. Some of 'em wouldn't think twice about working you over to find out what you was talking about."

"Some of 'em wouldn't include you, by any chance."

A set of Scandinavian-type features arranged themselves into a wounded expression. "Oakes is the closest thing I got to a family. Anyways, not one that smacks me around with a belt buckle and locks me in the basement with the rats and spiders. I took off half my skin crawling out a shoebox window. He found me, cleaned the shit off me, gave me a place to sleep. I been sleeping there sixteen months now."

"The Imperial Massage Parlor?"

"Yeah. I bunk with Py."

"Empty your pockets. Put everything on the dash."

He hesitated, then plundered his jacket and jeans and deposited it all in a row: a box of Marlboros, a disposable lighter, a department-store cell phone, an open package of condoms, and an old-fashioned-looking key on a ring. It looked like just the kind that would fit the front door of the old house in Jackson.

"Okay, put it back."

Stowing it away revived his confidence. "You believe me, uh?"

"For now. I left my portable polygraph in my other suit. What do they call you?"

"Dex."

"Go home, Dexter. Get a rubdown and tell Oakes thanks but nuts. Next time I see one of these skateboards I'll run it over, even if it scratches my undercarriage."

"I can't just go back empty-handed." His expression belonged to a wounded malamute.

"Tell him I'm going to Harper Woods. You beat it out of me." I kicked the magazine out of the pistol, shucked the shell from the chamber, pocketed the loads, and returned the pistol to the glove compartment. "Take me back to my car."

Back on Grand River he circled the block without being told, looking for lingering police activity. The closest thing to it was a parking ticket under my windshield wiper; the current administration was cracking down on derelict vehicles. The spectators were gone. I was wandering around, spreading blades of overgrown grass with my feet, when Fakim, the Chaldean proprietor, came out holding the Ruger by its handle between thumb and forefinger.

"You know, those things are what's wrong with this place," he said, when I took it back.

"I thought it was the weather." I made a quick inspection and put it back in its clip. "Sorry about your lawn." The Cutlass had scored two ruts in the grass.

"I think you should find someplace else to park."

"How much time can you give me?"

"Say to the end of the week." Apology dragged at the Mediterranean features. "I have expenses: taxes, health inspectors, city councilman on the cuff. I can't risk showing up in police reports."

"I used to feel the same way."

I got in. My key was still in the ignition. I started up and backed around behind the building, gentle as the crystal mist that was still falling down.

Dusk crept along the streets of Harper Woods and lay thick as ivy on the eastern exposure of George Hoyle's Tudor house. I wanted to hear straight from him the circumstances of his break with Paula Lawes,

195

and this time I left the velvet gloves behind.

The up-and-down, down-and-up tolling of the door chimes sounded like the BBC signing off during the Blitz. The sky had stopped weeping, but the occasional drop let go of a bare tree branch and struck the flagstone walk with a splat. While I was waiting I finished the cigarette I'd started in the car, then snapped it toward a puddle and pressed the button again. When that still got me nothing I tried the brass thumb latch. It responded without resistance and the door opened away from my fist.

Technically it was breaking and entering; all you have to do is move the door to qualify as a felon. I rapped on the frame, as much for good luck as to announce myself, said, "Hoyle?" That would look good on the signed statement.

It was probably my imagination, but the single syllable seemed to bounce off the walls of the large foyer like a tennis ball slowing to a stop, or a call inside a cave that had been vacant since the Neolithic.

I knew a chill of déjà vu. How many empty houses had I stood in and felt that same sensation? Big old piles with impressive dates carved into the lintel; bigger houses yet, smelling of fresh paint and new money; claustrophobic dumps with something scratching behind the lath-and-plaster; two-story condos carved out of reclaimed warehouses; tiny apartments reeking of cooked cabbage and worse, with greasy light switches and narrow aisles plowed through piles of yellowed newspapers, heaps of food containers, exhausted but populous, brambles of dried-out ballpoints, atolls of pet feces, broken toys, pieces of drywall, spilled insulation, carcinogens, and sometimes carcasses; products of some architect's hangover, indirectly lit, rooms that flowed into one another with no walls dividing them and no sign of anyone ever having trod the carpets or looked out the windows; cozy old farmhouses built by immigrants, with wood-burning stoves, Sears & Roebuck wallpaper, root cellars, potato bins, and barns out back twice their size; tidy houses, messy houses, overdecorated houses, houses furnished from yard sales and curbsides; *Jetsons*-style structures run entirely by satellite; ranch styles and A-frames, American Craftsman and saltbox, Victorian, Edwardian, Palladian, prefab; log, stucco, tile, clapboard, tin, cold marble, warm brick. Every kind of shelter, castles and wickiups not excluded. It's always the same. Like walking through the rib cage of a skeleton.

The living room with its trestle tables and tough leather upholstery looked like a museum exhibit, only without the ropes strung up to keep tourists away from the props. The iron chandelier was lit, the manufactured melting wax still awaiting its cue to drop, and the stag embroidered on the framed scrap of tapestry turning its head my way on its muscular neck, one hoof lifted, poised to run. In the hallway I passed the same ruffled women and tighted-and-leotarded men, frozen behind the murk some conscientious forger had applied to the canvases.

I heard a voice then, a masculine rumbling coming from near the end of the hall. Calm, measured tones. I eased the deep-bellied revolver back into its clip. I'd drawn it without being aware of it.

That made twice in one case my career pessimism had taken me off track. I needed a hobby, a diversion, a sports team I could root for and expect satisfaction. I needed to move to another city for that.

Outside the room where Hoyle tweaked the recordings of books, I paused to mop clammy sweat off my forehead with the back of my hand. Spools of magnetic tape turned slowly, propelling the placid manly mono-logue I'd heard from down the hall through the speaker, which wasn't any more visible than it had been the last time:

Elisa cast another glance toward the tractor shed. The strangers were getting into their Ford coupe. She took off a glove and put her strong fingers down into the forest of new green chrysanthemum sprouts that were growing around the old roots. . . .

Steinbeck. At least Hoyle wouldn't have an issue with the American accent.

He was there in his chair. He would be, and he wouldn't be any good to me now.

TWENTY-TWO

Stepping close, I bent down and turned my head sideways to face him on a level. The Lincolnesque face had lost much of its structure, the flesh bloated away from the strong bone superstructure. The escarpment of gray hair, formerly brushed aggressively into submission, hung in an arc over the side of his forehead nearest the pull of gravity. One of his long witchlike hands lay on the keyboard, the index finger crooked over the key labeled REVERB, as if he'd been interrupted in the midst of activating it.

A purplish hole marred the flat expanse of his exposed temple, puckered and blackened at the edges.

. . . It was a hard-swept looking little house, with hard-polished windows . . .

One of the row of metal switches that ran under the tape reels was out of line with the

200

others, slanting up toward the ceiling. After a moment's hesitation I reached up and tipped it down, using the back of a knuckle. The recitation stopped.

Hoyle was dressed much as he was during my first visit, in a plain shirt with the sleeves rolled past his forearms, chinos cinched with a woven leather belt, his feet stuck inside scuffed loafers, drawn up under his swivel chair, the way a man does when leaning into his work. Half his shirttail hung outside the slacks; but then while concentrating on the business at hand he wouldn't adjust his appearance to greet a visitor he probably didn't know was present.

That was guesswork, and as much detecting of his person as I cared to make. It had been a long time since I'd gotten satisfaction, personal or professional, from frisking a corpse.

I smelled it then. I don't know how I'd missed it, except maybe because I'd been around it often enough not to consider it unusual: the cap-pistol stench of spent powder, strong as ozone after a lightning strike. That spared me the chore of touching his skin to test its temperature. He hadn't been dead long enough for it to thin out.

The other thing it meant shouldn't have taken me as long to notice. It was on its way, blinking on in sequence like runway lights toward an approaching plane, when a current of air moved behind me and a bus struck me on the back of the head. Red and black filled my skull and I thought I smelled chrysanthemums; but that was probably John Steinbeck's fault. I don't know now if I had time to form that opinion before I left that sphere.

Swish-click! Swish-click!

I was dozing aboard a fast-moving train, racing across Canada or Europe or Asia; somewhere anyway where transit is rapid and the tracks are maintained on a regular basis. Surely not America. My head ached, probably from diesel exhaust, but that wasn't what I was smelling. It was an acrid odor of burned sulfur and cordite, the last thing I'd smelled before the bus hit me.

Swish-click!

I tried to open my eyes, but I hadn't the tools for the job. In lieu of a pinch bar and a chain fall I groped for my face with a pair of hands wrapped in boxer's gloves, came at last to the lids, and teased them open; a kneading operation, the opposite of closing the eyes of a cadaver.

The room I was in was a blur, but as my pupils expanded — slowly as water hollowing out a cavern — I saw George Hoyle's loafers, still on his feet in the position I'd last seen them in, only then from a higher angle. I was sitting on the floor of the room containing his control board, my back propped against the wall opposite the panel.

Swish-click! For some reason the noise was louder when I could see the source. Albert White, Allen Park Police Commander emeritus, stood leaning against the closed door to the hallway, ankles crossed, manipulating a steel baton, a cop staple that folded into a compact package by way of a steel cylinder sliding into a hollow sleeve, like a car radio antenna, only sturdier and designed to inflict as much damage as the wielder cared to inflict; in this case a love pat on my cerebellum.

In ruthless or inexpert hands, even that could put the victim in a coma or kill him outright. In my case, surviving with my senses more or less intact was a combination of skill on his part and decades of calcium buildup where others had struck me in the same general location, with everything from blackjacks to pistol butts to high heels. I reached back with a clumsy paw. My scalp was tender to the touch, but he hadn't broken the skin. When it came to blunt instruments he was a maestro. I let the hand drop.

White was dressed in his retiree's uniform: starched denim shirt, slacks with pleats, brown shoes, old but polished. His crew cut, which he must have freshened once a week, was as level as the top of a flathead screw and his eyes glittered far back in their wrinkled sockets. His smile showed only his lower teeth, supported by the square pillar of his cleft chin.

"Go ahead," he said. "It's not my carpet."

I leaned over and vomited. It was mostly liquid. I smelled stale Scotch and staler tobacco; groped for a handkerchief, but my thick fingers couldn't find the pocket. I wiped my mouth on my coat sleeve.

"A little out of your jurisdiction, aren't you?"

Whoever asked the question was trying to give an impression of my voice, but it came out as garbled as a flight announcement at the airport.

He swish-clicked the baton again, extending the business end with a flip of the wrist, then collapsing it with the palm of his free hand. His tongue bulged his pale slack cheek, deciding whether to answer.

"That's one of the advantages of getting

204

yourself busted down to private citizen," he said. "All the fences come down."

"How long was I out?"

"Three, four minutes. I didn't time it." He lifted the baton again.

I put out a hand before he could shoot it open. "Put that down, will you? Or hit me again so I don't have to hear it."

For a second he seemed to consider that. I reminded myself next time not to think with my mouth. Finally he laid the weapon on the control board. He pushed himself upright, fists hanging, kicked at something with a foot. Blue steel and glistening brown wood spun my way across the carpet, like a bottle in a kissing game: a .38 revolver. It had been lying under the dead man's chair. If it had been there when I'd come in I hadn't noticed. Maybe it was the one I'd seen before in Hoyle's drawer; but they all look alike apart from the serial number. "Pick it up."

I shook my head. My brain slid on a cushion of fluid, coming to rest against the wall of my skull and making my eyes water.

Something turned over with a crunch, like a sluggish engine. It was what he would call a chuckle. He raised his hands to his shoulders, palms forward. "I'm not going to shoot you in self-defense," he said. "Too many cops have ruined that for the rest of us. Pick it up. It's not loaded. I made sure of that before I put it back down."

"If you want my fingerprints to be found on it, you're going to have to put them there yourself."

I shifted my weight from one hip to the other, as if I was getting a sore spot. I was; but I wanted to assure myself the Ruger was in its clip. I felt the solid lump of it when I leaned that way.

He wasn't fooled. "It's there. What makes you think I didn't make sure of that too?"

"Why did I kill him? I just woke up and I'm fuzzy on the details."

Retirement hadn't slowed him down. He had the baton in his right hand before I saw him move. I managed to throw up my arm just as it swung around. The solid steel core struck bone. My forearm went dead to the elbow.

The bottom-feeding smile stayed in place as he watched me rubbing my arm. The baton hung at his side. "Don't try that shit on me, disarming the enemy with blinding wit. I practically invented it. What happened here was an accident. The piece is Hoyle's. He pulled it on you while you were pumping him about what happened to Paula Lawes. You fought him for it and won —

only you didn't, really, because he died before you could get any answers."

"So that's what happened. I'm your stand-in."

"It's messy, sure. Name a crime scene that isn't."

I shook my arm. Circulation marched up alongside the bone on tiny hobnailed boots. "What's Paula Lawes to you?"

He raised the baton again. I shrank back against the wall, but he let it drop at the end of his fist, still showing his teeth. "She means about as much to me as the starving Africans. I wanted to hear from Hoyle what he knew about Marcus Root."

"What makes you think he knew anything?"

"He was awful convincing the other times we talked." He stooped to snatch the .38 off the floor where it had fallen when my arm gave out. "It's got to be this way, to fit the crime scene. It'd look more natural if you put on the prints yourself, but even the forensics wonks like to get home at a decent hour. I don't guess they'll kick up a fuss." A gray tongue slid along the top of his lowers. "Sorry I can't make it clean and quick. Your heart had to keep pumping just long enough to snatch the gun from him and put a slug in his brain." He stuck the baton under one arm, fished a handful of shells from his pocket, and loaded the cylinder, placing spent ones in the last two chambers. "Liver ought to do it. You'd have maybe twenty minutes." He swung the cylinder into place, cocked the hammer, and aimed at a spot on my right side just above the belt.

It wasn't a chance at all, really; especially with my arm still out of commission. But even a cornered animal will lash out. I leaned forward, changing my center of gravity, braced myself against the floor with both hands flat on the carpet, and swept my left foot up and sideways, hoping to hook his ankle.

No, it was no chance at all. The report of the gun in that small room was as loud as Krakatoa.

TWENTY-THREE

My eyes opened this time without resistance.

Hell was pretty much what I'd expected: no lake of fire, no furnaces to stoke, no round-the-clock barbershop quartets with accordion accompaniment, just the prospect of spending an eternity in the very place where I'd made my last mistake.

I was still sitting on the floor of George Hoyle's recording studio, my head still expanding and contracting with each heartbeat, with the bonus of a high-pitched ringing in my ears and my nostrils stinging from a fresh infusion of spent powder; that sulfur stink at least was true to the Old Testament.

It came with a demon: eight feet of Chinese mythology in the same washed-out blue T-shirt and baggy green cargo pants I'd seen somewhere in life, although I couldn't place where just yet. It stood inside the doorway, stooped to clear the ceiling, and enough to the side for another vaguely familiar figure to insert itself into my damnation. The chrome steel Howitzer, which had seemed in proportion to its carrier when the giant had held it, looked as big as the jawbone of an ass in Oakes Steadman's hand.

It wasn't smoking; modern loads don't. But in my heightened state of awareness the big muzzle looked hot, as if an orange-red glow had just faded away.

"I replaced the firing pin." He unchambered a handful of shells and held the gun across his body for Py to take.

Py. Things were coming back to me in shards, like ancient pottery. I had only to fit them together to know what had taken place. All I needed was a good light and a new head.

Five people were as many as the room could hold, even if two of them weren't in a position to bump into anything. Albert White lay on his face at George Hoyle's feet, his hand still wrapped around the .38 revolver with the arm flung out to his side. Miraculously — comically — the baton was still clamped under his other arm, like a British officer's riding crop in a war film. The .44 magnum had turned the back of his head into a soup bowl filled with red blood and gray matter.

The big man accepted the weapon the way an infant closes its fist around a rattle for the first time, not knowing what to do with it. Steadman grasped his wrist with one hand, tightened the other around the hand holding the gun, and inserted his finger in the trigger guard.

Anticipating, I stuck my fingers in my ears. The drums will take only so much punishment before they stop performing.

The former gang-banger had left one un-fired round in the cylinder. Muted as it sounded, the roar still shook the room. A star of plaster leapt from the wall a couple of feet above my head, letting a tendril of pale batting escape through the hole. Hoyle had soundproofed the room all around.

What his bodyguard had anticipated, I couldn't tell. He'd fallen against the wall at his back and would have dropped the big revolver if Steadman hadn't still been hold-ing his hand.

"Sorry, Py," he said. "They're gonna test you, and I can't be handling no guns. Remind me to wash my hands," he told me.

Today it was a scarlet-and-black Red Wings warm-up jacket zipped to his neck and gray whipcord trousers stuffed into the tops of his lace-up boots. He wore a cap with the Red Wings logo at the required angle, with the bill cocked over his left ear, with his dreads spilling like tentacles out the bottom.

"Dex called you," I said. "You made good time coming all the way from Jackson."

"We was in Inkster: Trooper there got into a hole trying to bust what he thought was a fence operation. Turned out it was storage for a gang-sponsored charity rummage sale. His sergeant thought I had a better chance of shooing away that mob than a riot squad. When Dex told me where you was headed, I knew sooner or later you'd stumble into Albert White."

"So White's the reason for my babysitter; not your old friends in the gang."

"They don't like me much, but now they got religion, me and who I hang out with ain't what you'd call a priority. Oh, they lay down scores, peddle dope, burn things, but considering my present circumstances and what I know about them, deals like this here are few and far between." He cocked an elbow toward the dead men.

"What was White's beef with Hoyle?"

He corked a thin smile by placing a finger to his lips. Turning a little, he found a switch out of line with the others and flicked it down. A second pair of tape reels stopped turning; I hadn't noticed them. He browsed the controls, found a rectangular handle, twisted it left. The reels started up again, faster than before, reversing directions. After a few seconds he stopped them, using the switch, then twisted the handle right.

". . . got to be this way, to fit the crime scene. It'd look more natural if you put on the prints yourself, but —"

Steadman stopped the tape. With White dead on the floor, his voice coming from the invisible speaker laid an icicle alongside my spine.

"You done that?" Steadman tilted his head toward the switches. "Smart."

"Unobservant. Hoyle must have been duping the reel I switched off. I didn't notice the other one turning."

"Dumb luck still counts. It'll clear up questions when I face the shooting board in Lansing. You'll sign a statement?"

"I'll sign my firstborn child over to you. But what about White and Hoyle?"

Smiling still, he looked at a spot above my head: the sound-deadening insulation hanging out of the bullethole. "Couldn't have picked a better place myself for all this gun stuff," he said. "We shouldn't have no interruptions." He stepped across White's body and extended a hand. I took it and together we got me up onto my feet. I stumbled, caught my balance with a hand on the back of Hoyle's chair. It made a quarter turn, dislodging his hand from the board. It dropped past the arm of the chair, swaying in mid-air.

The former gang member sneered down at him. "Always happens. They crack the till and come up with a fistful of shit. You'd think they'd learn."

He left the room, Py backing out behind him with the magnum, empty now of ammunition, pointing at me. He'd need a calm steady voice and diagrams to understand what had taken place; but then so would I. I followed them down the hall into the living room.

TWENTY-FOUR

Only one lamp burned in the room, which helped complete the medieval effect. I wandered over to one of the big distressed-leather sofas, concentrating on not limping, and lowered myself onto it without making any extraneous noise. That scraped the bottom of my stores of energy.

Steadman remained standing. "Where's the man keep his booze, do you think?"

I inventoried the room, lighting on an oaken cabinet with fittings of verdigreed brass. "What are the odds Pope Julius stored his Gutenbergs there?"

"Some things don't change. Guy makes himself some jack, the days of the old serf system start to look good. Py, whyn't you mix us up a coupla highballs?" He looked at me. "Don't stare. If he'd stopped at six feet, he could be running the show in the Hyatt lounge."

"Everybody's good at something," I said.

"I'll find mine someday. Don't speak so ill of the dead. Hoyle said he rented the place furnished."

"No disrespect intended. You've seen my crib. Had my way, it'd be Danish Modern. We got the same climate."

The giant threaded his magnum under his waistband and bent double to open the door to the cabinet. The shelves were stocked with premium brands. He transferred two tall gold-veined glasses to the top, selected a bottle of Gentleman Jack and a leaded-glass seltzer jug, and went to work.

"Man must have some ice in the kitchen," Steadman said.

"I came in here to drink, not skate."

Py lived up to his hype. He filled the glasses two thirds of the way, topped them off with a squirt, and clinked a long-handled spoon inside the concoction, all with a minimum of fuss. He brought mine over with a paper cocktail napkin wrapped around it and handed Steadman his. The gang consultant leaned against a wall and sipped. So far I'd never seen him sit.

Py seemed content to stay on his feet as well. The twelve-foot ceiling suited him. He let his arms hang to his sides as if he didn't know what else to do with them.

"Lansing's had White under investigation

for eighteen months," Steadman said. "The joint savings account he shares with his wife takes a hit of several thousand bucks four times a year, going back almost seven years. Coincidentally enough, George Hoyle's checking account goes up roughly the same within a week of each of White's withdrawals. Not the exact same, of course; folks hold out walking-around money. Anyway as patterns go this one's louder than a Christmas tie. In this here cashless society we got, blackmail leaves a paper trail you could stub your toe on."

I drank. The big Chinese was wasted watching the other's back. I'd watched him make the drinks, but I knew I could duplicate every move and not come close. "How'd the state police get a court order to tap into their accounts?"

White had said the former gang member had diamonds in his teeth. He showed me one above the rim of his glass. "One perk of not being swore in as an officer is you don't have to deal with judges and such. I still got some friends on the street. You think we ain't progressed beyond zip guns and switchblades?"

"Fly on the wall."

"Say what?"

"What I'd like to have been in the commander's office in Lansing when you pitched having an old crony hack into a retired cop's financial records."

"My old man said it's easier to ask forgiveness than permission; 'course, he died in stir. I had the printouts.

"I never thought the rot in the Allen Park Police Department stopped with Marcus Root," he went on. "We found enough knickknacking all along the chain of command to seat a grand jury, but with White we hit the mother lode. Question was what was he paying to keep quiet?"

"Seven years," I said. "Paula Lawes?"

He shook his head. "Marcus Root."

I took another sip. Compared to what I was hearing the bourbon had no more kick than Gatorade. I waited.

"Based on what we delivered in Lansing, the Jackson post got the go-ahead to crack the P.D. records in Allen Park. We didn't know just what we was looking for, so that took months, including going back over what we read looking to see what fit and what didn't.

"Two days after Root was killed, the civilian employee in charge of the police impound lot reported a discrepancy in the mileage recorded on a 'sixty-eight Plymouth Duster seized during a drug raid when it was parked and when the employee took a routine inventory first of the month: Somehow while the car was sitting in the lot it managed to rack up an additional eight and sixth-tenths of a mile. That's roughly the round-trip to the crime scene and back. The car was a low-rider, chopped by a kid waiting in a cell for his case to come up at County."

I leaned forward and set my glass on the heavy table in front of me. My hand shook a little, but that could have been fatigue; the day was wearing on. It wasn't fatigue.

Steadman helped himself to another sip, licked his lips. He was enjoying himself, but he'd had more time to digest the information. "Root was more careful than his boss. We never found anything in his records to back up what us homies knew about how he squoze us. He probably stashed it in cash, someplace it won't show up till somebody tears down a house or moves a statue in the park. There was some substantial healthy activity in White's account from time to time that didn't jibe with his commander's pay, so we know he and Root had a partnership deal. We can't prove it, but now we won't have to. What exactly convinced him to kill Root, whether Root wanted a bigger slice of the pie or got religion and wanted to spill everything to Internal Affairs, we'll never know. But thanks to that tape, we can prove he killed Hoyle.

"The impound wasn't guarded that night," he continued. "Detroit's bankruptcy at the time trickled down to most of the suburbs, leading to cost-saving measures. White borrowed the car, knowing that would make it look like one of us did it. Probably he got the squeal on Paula Lawes, so he knew right where to find Root, do him, and take his notebook so it would look like the cases were connected. The more mud you stir up in an investigation, the harder it is to clear it up."

"But what could Hoyle know that was worth paying him all these years to keep quiet?"

The diamond vanished behind a frown. "That we don't know, but he must have had evidence of some kind. Anyway we'll hook up with the Harper Woods cops and take this place apart brick by brick if we got to. One thing I found out working this side of the fence is file clerks don't like folders flapping open."

"If White could have finished Hoyle anytime, why choose today?"

"You scared him. Digging into the Lawes

disappearance, which happened the same night as Root's death, you might turn up something. He's probably been planning this for some time, figuring to get him to cough up what he had — that baton's a persuader, I can tell you from experience — but you helped him make up his mind to act when he did. Hoyle spoiled things by throwing down on him, but then you showed up and gave him just the fall guy he needed. Once you and Hoyle killed each other while you were pumping him, he hoped like us to find what he was after by searching the place."

I looked at Py, to see if he was buying any of this any more than I was, but he wasn't present. He was staring somewhere into the middle distance between himself and the Sea of Japan. "That's another one I owe you, if that pile of by-guess-and-by-God pans out. I had you cold for Root."

"That was my fault. You were fucking up my case." Steadman took another hit, swallowed, stood his glass on the heavy fireplace mantel. "I don't like the odds either. We'll see what White's widow has to say. Her name's on that account too. They been married too long for him to make up stories about good days crawling the casinos."

"Cop's wife," I said. "Good luck with that."

All the stars were wrapped in black cotton when I got away from there. The Harper Woods police were clerkly in their approach to a little thing like violent death, got my story and Steadman's — as much as they applied to the crime scene, minus extraneous details like the specific investigations that had brought us to Hoyle in the first place — and my promise to drop by headquarters and sign my name to what amounted to perjury by omission. If St. Peter keeps tabs on police blotters, I might as well save myself the trip.

My house had a shut-up smell, as if I'd been gone a week. I could live with that; I was too wiped out to open a bottle, much less a window. Unpacking my personal gear in the bedroom, I checked the cylinder in the Ruger. All the chambers were loaded. White had run a bluff, not that I'd been in a position to throw down on him, sitting on the floor with him standing over me and the Seven Dwarfs swinging pickaxes at my skull. That was a dull ache now, running tenth place behind every muscle in my body and a leg that would never heal completely. I stripped to my shorts, threw myself on top

222

of the blankets, and was leagues under when Doc, Grumpy, and company traded their picks for sledges and set them clanging against raw ore. I swung my feet over the side of the mattress, groping my grouty scalp with both hands and waiting for the ringing to stop.

It wouldn't do that, not until I caromed my way into the living room and lifted the telephone receiver off the cradle.

"Wake you?" Alderdyce asked.

"No. I'm still asleep."

"Good." He wasn't listening. Cops don't when it's just social intercourse. "I'm reconsidering your proposal of marriage. That ring you gave me is one of a kind."

Somebody was breathing, drawing long ragged breaths. They were mine. I waited.

"Yeah," he said, as if I'd responded. "This won't play over the wire. You know where I live?"

TWENTY-FIVE

I'd known John Alderdyce for nearly a biblical span, since we'd replayed every episode of *Combat* and *The Gallant Men* with sticks and cap pistols in various alleys, but I couldn't remember the last time I'd been to his house.

There were a number of reasons for that, one in particular.

There's nothing wrong with Redford Township, if living there was your decision. The school dropout rate's lower than in many of the local districts and the crime statistics aren't as high as in, say, Dearborn, just a few blocks south; one characteristic of the local lowlife is it observes natural breaks, as rain does when it falls habitually on one side of the street while the sun shines on the other. The same chain restaurants you see everywhere else are conveniently located, and the residents know which ones are reliable and which haven't been monitored by the franchiser since Colonel Sanders was a buck private. There's everything to recommend the place, except when you have no other choice.

When the Alderdyces moved in, the Detroit Police Department required its personnel to live inside the city limits, which chained them to the brick box they'd called home for more than thirty years; a nice enough house, but not their first choice, or even their second. No matter what they did to it, for them it would have all the personal character of a factory house.

When the restriction was lifted finally, it was too late. They'd raised their two sons, seen them off to start their own families, and paid off the mortgage. There was no point in tossing a police inspector's pension and semiretirement income down another hole that no bank in the world would give them another thirty years to fill in, so here they were and here they'd stay until the deep stranger came to their door.

Accepting the situation, Marilee Alderdyce had decked the place out with the patient care of a passionate homemaker, a skilled occupation, and one she nailed. Ivory-colored curtains shimmered in the windows and copper chimes hung from the eaves, chanting gentle hymns when the breeze tickled them. As I climbed the front stoop, a security bulb clacked on, frosting the plants set out in window boxes in chilly white light. They were dormant, but when spring decided to put in an appearance they would explode into domes of Kodachrome color like aerial footage of a bombing run.

There was no bell, just a stirrup-shaped knocker that didn't look as if it had ever been used. I bare-knuckled the panel. Marilee opened the door almost before I could lower my hand. A tall woman, medium-dark, reddish highlights in her hair, which swept forward in twin points at the corners of her jaw; high cheekbones and eyes the color of cherrywood. A powder-blue top with a boatneck collar — usually avoided by women her age — exposed few lines in her long neck. She was slim-hipped in gray slacks and her feet were long and narrow in gray Topsiders. She greeted me in a tone cool as mist — not hostile; almost cordial, in fact — and stood aside for me to get in past her.

She didn't care for me. Why this was I couldn't quite fix to a certainty, and wouldn't ask. It may have had to do with my dropping out of the Detroit Police training course a week short of finishing, or because I was the one who'd talked John into signing up for it with me in the first place. Possibly it was a combination of both, although I leaned toward the second. Every time she swept a floor she hadn't picked out, or pulled a weed from the garden she'd planted to cover the concrete foundation that should have been fieldstone, it'd be me she thought of. You have to put a face on a blame, and mine was the only one that didn't change.

I found John in the mudroom at the back of the house, where he got up from what looked like the same padded hydraulic chair he'd used for years in his old office at 1300 Beaubien to shake my hand. The place smelled of laundry detergent and corn-starch. Here, in a workspace he'd set up opposite a washer-dryer set and an ironing board supporting a succession of dress shirts in every color, a fat venerable CTR monitor sat on a some-assembly-required computer desk, facing a wall newly plastered with the family photos he'd stuffed into his carton when he gave Reliance his notice. At home, he dressed more like a regular person and less like a model for the Men's Wear-house, in a Wayne State University sweat-shirt, khaki trousers, and black sneakers. The homey surroundings and weekend clothes brought his brutally hacked-out features into stark relief.

The monitor on the desk — flat white, with a bulbous screen — was so far out of date it looked like a prop from a Molly Ringwald movie. The image on the screen-saver was the arched façade of 1300, the old Detroit Police Headquarters, inspired by the prison-palaces of Venice during the Inquisition. He wouldn't have put himself out to download it: Along with the office chair he'd appropriated the computer and everything that came with it, down to a stapler heavy enough to double as a black-jack; which most likely it had in gentler times.

He caught me looking. "The chief said I was welcome to carry anything away I wanted. He had the computer scrubbed of everything sensitive. Saved the department the expense of carting it all to the dump. City's more interested in fixing up the old Michigan Central train station than it is in keeping a roof over its police force."

"Maybe the Chinese'll buy the place, make a matched set with all the others." I reached for my cigarettes, then changed my mind. I could never keep track of when he was smoking and when he was quitting. "Tell me about the ring. You've made me the happiest man on earth, by the way.

Where should we go for the honeymoon?"

He sat down without answering or inviting me to sit. Here at last was the Alderdyce I knew. I drew up a chair with a folding step stool built into it and used it while he took something from a drawer in the desk. He leaned back, holding the ring I'd given him by the band, suitor style.

"I rousted out half a dozen fences from the old days," he said, "reliable snitches. Some of them were retired, they said, but they stood in their doorways looking like I couldn't blast 'em loose with dynamite. Not my concern now, if it ever was; the boys in B-and-E can look after their own. I even talked to your boy Orbit."

That gave me pause until I remembered Harry Lauder, the current alias, belonged to Eugene Orbit, the fence I'd gone to in quest of information on the ring some magpie had decided to deposit on my kitchen table. "I'm sure he was helpful."

"No worse than some. No better, for sure; but you learn to read between the lies. I figure the dope he gave me was straight; if you stretch the term. Anyway he pointed me in some directions.

"I won't give up my snitches even now, but the one that rang the bell led me to an old friend in Robbery Armed, who worked a crash-and-grab job that went down back when Archer was mayor. You know the M.O. in those scores."

"Uh-huh." Like everything else that originated in Detroit, the procedure added horsepower to the old smash-and-grab: Instead of invading a store on foot and shattering the glass display cases, our pioneers steal a truck, ram it through the front door, jump out, shovel the swag into the bed, and blow. It's more scientific than it sounds; the ones that aren't busted right away have cased the precinct for weeks, breaking windows and kicking in doors for show, noting the police response times, arriving at an average, and on the big night are in and out in half that, leaving behind what they can't fit into the schedule.

"This one was more sophisticated than most," Alderdyce said. "They bought the truck secondhand, cash, no paperwork; size of the score, I guess they didn't want to chance getting picked up on the way. The place was called Monte Carlo's, in Southfield. It was a clearinghouse for several mall chains, tons of wholesale merch in a safe sunk in a yard of concrete. They just jerked it out with a chain and took it with 'em. We found it in the ditch they dumped it in after blowing it at their leisure. Going by photos of the jewels provided by the owner, R/A and the FBI traced the stuff to fence operations in Minnesota, Texas, and California, recovered a lot of it but by no means all, and got some convictions. This" — he gestured with the ring — "was one of the items that weren't recovered. Routinely, those strays are bought by private parties for cash, no names attached. They're the toughest to find. Whoever made you the beneficiary of this one gave us a break."

"You think Frances Lawes proposed with a hot rock?"

"The rich didn't get that way by not recognizing a bargain when they saw it."

I said, "He'd argue the rich part. According to his press he works on salary, like everyone else at City Hall."

"And yet everyone who leaves that building for the last time retires to some island in the tropics."

I didn't bother to field that one. Wondering how people who are smarter than I am turn everything they touch to gold lost its appeal a long time ago.

"Receiving stolen property is a couple of football fields away from murder," I said.

"It would explain why he refused to identify the ring as the one he gave his missing wife." He huffed on the diamond, buffed it on his shirt. "So much for your theory it proved he didn't kill her because recovering it would reopen the investigation into her disappearance."

I shifted my weight on the metal chair, shifted it back when the Ruger dug a hole in my hip. I'd become so accustomed to packing iron on this case I'd clean forgotten I was entering a career cop's house lugging an unregistered handgun.

I shook my head, as much to distract his attention from the maneuver as to refute what he'd said. Just because he was retired didn't mean he wouldn't blow the whistle on me on a charge of insulting his hospitality. "Doesn't hold water. The statute of limitations on a robbery charge would have run out years ago."

"Not if it linked him to another murder."

Smug wasn't an emotion in John Alderdyce's toolbox. He'd stared down too many grand juries to have use for it. But as I said, I've known the man since sticks and cap pistols. He fingered the ring in both hands, admiring the way the harsh overhead light in the laundry flashed off the facets, reflecting off the walls and ceiling like a disco ball.

"The bookkeeper at Monte Carlo's was

232

working late that night, trying to account for thirty-five cents in cash receipts that weren't in the ledger. When he came running out of the back room, thinking a tornado had hit, the perp behind the wheel stepped on the gas and pinned him to a wall. The driver and his accomplices grabbed what they could, then tore into reverse, leaving the bean-counter still pasted to the Sheetrock. He died at Receiving the next day. Internal injuries. Don't know if his employers ever solved the mystery of the extra thirty-five cents.

"It's the police equivalent of a throw-out at home plate," he went on, "avoiding an RBI. If we can't get him life for Paula, we can snag five to ten for accessory after the fact to Felony Homicide."

He turned in the swivel and tossed the ring onto the desk. "Ever have one of those days that start out shitty and wind up like Christmas morning? I may have lost my job, but I gained a collar. Thanks, Santa."

TWENTY-SIX

"Don't set out the milk and cookies just yet," I said. "To make stick a charge of receiving you have to prove the defendant knew it was hot, which is where those things usually blow up. Say you clear that hurdle; then to beat the statute of limitations you have to prove he knew there was a murder involved. That'd be like winning the lottery twice in a row. No prosecutor worth his pinstripes would touch it. If it blew up, the whole case would fall apart like government housing."

That brought him close to tears — and there was peace in the Middle East. "Did I say I was finished? San Diego P.D. raided a roach motel a week after the score, a place that specializes in guests waiting for the all-clear to jump the Mexican border: No name in the register in return for room rates that'd make the manager of the Waldorf choke on his goose liver. We've got the same thing here on Jefferson, different border. Well, it was a good day's catch. Along with a bent commodities broker, a couple of cocaine cowboys, and a road-show Kevorkian who strangled his terminal wife to death with her pantyhose, the Dago cops bagged one Allen Zog, known to the pack he hung with on West Michigan as Albanian Al; his common-law wife sold him out when he forgot to split his share of the take with her before he split, period. His prints were all over the truck that turned Monte Carlo's into Mount St. Helens when we found it abandoned in the warehouse district.

"Jury hardly left the box," he said. "Thirty years in Marquette. I don't know our current headhunter in office personally, but if he runs to type, that sparkler could put the Zogster back behind the wheel, delivering fresh headaches to my former employers. How's that for your diamond in the rough?"

"Provided he cooperates." I was counting on my fingers. "Provided he was there when Lawes bought the ring, and provided he can testify Lawes knew the circumstances. All of which hinges on whether he even bought the ring. You can't establish if he's the one who had it engraved or someone else named Frances intended it for someone else named Paula. If all that doesn't gum up the wheels of justice, your star witness is a convicted felon who'd pimp his sister to get out of Marquette." I ran out of fingers and put them to use fishing out a cigarette; I should care about his sensibilities any more than he did mine. But I didn't light it.

"I didn't say it didn't need homework. I got all the time in the world, thanks to you. Now I can draw unemployment."

I stuck out my hand. "Gimme back my ring."

"Nope. It belongs to the insurance company."

"I'll put it in safekeeping till they come to claim it. I've got as much right to it as you; maybe more. You're not a cop anymore. You're not even a private detective."

"What do you want with it?"

"I might want to propose to someone."

He reached back without looking, scooped up the ring, juggled it in his palm. "This is the only evidence I've got. How do I know you won't throw it in the river to protect your client?"

"The same way I know you won't hire a couple of Zog's fellow inmates to bounce his head off the shower tiles till he agrees to implicate Lawes."

I kept my hand out all this time. He bounced the bauble once more, then leaned forward and dropped it into my palm. "Don't put it in that cheese box in your office," he said. "I could crack it with a blunt word."

"I'll take out a safety-deposit box." I dandled it a couple of times myself, then recovered the scrap of tissue, retwisted it inside, and put it in my inside pocket. I made the decision then I'd been playing with. "You'll hear some gossip from your friends in the department about a cop killing in Harper Woods. Retired cop, not that that counts in your crowd."

"Albert White. I heard already." He tilted his massive head toward a police-band scanner murmuring on a shelf next to a stack of towels, another piece of office plunder. "I was hoping I wouldn't have to be the one who brought it up. I feel a little better now about giving up the ring. Let's hear your side."

I blew a jet of smoke. I didn't remember lighting up. "I went back to George Hoyle's — you remember him, during the Paula Lawes investigation you gave him a break on his extracurricular activities — to pick up some sticks I missed the first time. He was no help, having been shot to death in the room where he edited his recorded books. Next thing I knew I was on the floor at his feet with a bump on my head courtesy of White, who was no slouch with a baton. How can I get one of those, by the way?"

"You can't. Stop picking daisies."

"Okay, I'll skip the dialogue. It'll all come out anyway; but I'll get to that. He laid out a plan to hang Hoyle's murder around my neck, which I took as a confession; not that I could do anything with it after I went on the record as killed in the shoot-out with Hoyle. That was the plan, anyway, only fate intervened. It's on tape, every word: happy accident. That's the part I was saving." I took another drag, pinched out the butt, and parked it in a pant cuff. "This next part is just mudroom gossip until the party involved makes his own statement."

"I'll put on the tea."

"Oakes Steadman, remember him?"

"I'm an elephant where his kind is concerned. Proceed."

"He may change your mind. He pinned a tail on me after we met; strictly for my protection, he said later. He and his shadow, a Chinese who could peek over the Great Wall on tiptoe, got there in time to put a bullet in White before he put one in me. According to Steadman, White and Marcus Root, the Allen Park officer who was killed not long after finding Paula Lawes's abandoned car, were shaking down the local gangs. Hoyle may have known something about that; Steadman thinks he knew something worse. When I started turning over old rocks, White got spooked and did Hoyle. This wasn't a new strategy. Steadman's evidence implicates White in Root's murder, another hush-up job."

"So why didn't Steadman move on White before he got to Hoyle?"

"The root — no pun intended — of 'implicate' is 'imply.' What he had, unexplained extra mileage on a low-rider that was supposed to be still under glass in the police impound, wouldn't get him an indictment, much less a conviction. Whatever Hoyle knew might, which is why the ex-commander paid him a visit, armed with a baton to beat out of him what he knew, whether he had proof, and where he had it, and a gun to finish him off afterwards. But Hoyle had a revolver and put up a fight that ended with him being killed with the wrong gun. That complicated the scenario, but it wasn't anything White couldn't work with. My wandering in when I did gave him a patsy: everything as it happened, only I was the one who struggled with Hoyle, and we both wound up dead with matching bullets."

I stopped to take in air. "I hope you're getting all this. I may need prompting when it comes time to dictate a statement."

Alderdyce leaned back, resting an elbow on the desk. His expressions changed as often as a solar eclipse.

"I'd give you an argument," he said, "or I would have, when I was still in harness. Being a civilian alters your perspective. It's no longer my responsibility to defend the thin blue line. I've seen my share of dirty cops, and more than my share of cover-ups. I had my doubts about White when we worked the Lawes case; nothing you could take to the spooks at IAD, but you don't roll with skunks and come up smelling like Old Spice. What did Hoyle tell you about Marcus Root's connection to Paula Lawes?"

"Only what he saw, or what he said he saw, in an Allen Park dive called the Gamesman Inn. Know it?"

"I knew it before I interviewed Hoyle about their relationship. The department keeps tabs on all the places in the metropolitan area where the pavement princesses meet their johns, especially when the john gives her a lift across the city line. No secret it's municipal policy to catch and release the pros, charge their male escorts, seize any cars employed in the offense against

240

decency, and sell 'em at auction. That leaves the girls on the street to troll for more contributors to the slush fund."

I hung another cigarette on my lip. "Shame on you. City making a comeback and all."

"What did Hoyle see in the Gamesman? It's cleaned up its act, by the way. Same name, different management. It's a real sports bar now: Sip your six-dollar beer and watch the Lions lose on ten flatscreen TVs."

"That's one of the things I went to his house to ask him about. One of Paula's friends said Paula cried on her shoulder over Hoyle's dumping her, a detail he overlooked the first time we spoke. He said Root — or a cop I would like to have been Root, since it would tie the two cases — came to their table and had a conversation with her that Hoyle couldn't make out, apart from that it seemed pleasant. If he forgot to tell me how things ended with Paula, he might also have forgotten what he did hear that night."

When Alderdyce nodded his head, it was like the Matterhorn shifting. "If he could connect Albert White to the Root killing, that conversation becomes important."

"Steadman stayed behind to see what he

241

could turn. Maybe Hoyle wrote something down."

"Or took pictures with a zoom lens and high-speed film. I mean, as long as we're dreaming. You trust this guy?"

"At this point I'd look for some way to alibi him out of a mass-murder charge backed up on CNN in living color. In this day and age I don't think there's any fate worse than death. Especially mine."

"You were out like the cat when White's ticket got punched. You sure it was Steadman's big stooge that did it? A convicted felon in possession of a firearm gets a direct flight back to the steel stable."

"All I can tell you is I saw it in Py's hand; Py, that's his official security. Even a mitt as big as his couldn't palm a forty-four magnum with an eight-inch barrel so it's out of sight."

"That's all you can tell me, huh."

"I wasn't so groggy I couldn't repeat it on the stand."

"And you'd alibi him out of a mass-murder charge in living color."

"Did I say that? It doesn't sound like me."

He stood, making none of the noises a retiree usually makes when getting upright. "Go home. You're groggier than you think."

"You're the one got me out of bed. It

could've waited till tomorrow. You just needed someone to crow to about nailing Francis X. Lawes."

"Just make sure that ring winds up in a safe place. After that, you're officially between cases."

I rose, making all the noises he'd neglected. I peeled the cigarette from my lip — it was dry, as they always were when I met in closed session with John Alderdyce — and poked it back into the pack. "Not from where I stand," I said. "Lawes hired me to prove whether Paula's dead or alive. Everything else I've accomplished so far is a sideshow. That belongs to your friends on the force. From now on I'm performing in the center ring."

"So does a clown."

He stuck out his hand. I shook it. On rainy days I can still feel his grip.

TWENTY-SEVEN

No mind is ever at rest. Even in sleep, Albert White's square head came between me and the light, his nasty length of steel slapping his thigh and his hand wrapped around the gun he'd used to kill George Hoyle, its muzzle trained on my chest. As if that wasn't enough, a rat or some other burrowing animal kept gnawing at my side, trying to make a hole for itself between ribs.

I sat up straight as an L brace. My brain was crystal clear. I knew what the animal was and why it had been pestering me all that long, long day. I exploded out from under the covers and made for the telephone in the living room.

The clock my grandfather had bought for his mother was knocking on heaven's door: knocking loud. The noises it made between strokes sounded like an old man coughing things loose from his lungs. When the last stroke came — there were twelve, what else?

— I walked away from the phone. It was too late to call; not from courtesy, but because this was a conversation that needed to take place in person and to call first would give the party all night to cook up a convincing lie.

In any case, I had another stop to make first; one that needed a night's rest and a fresh outlook. I went back to bed, but I didn't get much rest, and the outlook was as stale as a celebrity roast.

Sometime in the early hours the climate had shifted gears, warming the earth and whipping yesterday's glacial rain into a lead-colored froth that cut the visibility back to my hood ornament and made the stretch between stoplights feel like paddling the wrong way up the Amazon. If the morning commuter traffic — never more than a crawl — slowed down any more it would be going backwards. The sun was a bloodshot eye, giving neither warmth nor cheer, and the potato-chip-thin ice in the potholes made crunching sounds when my tires broke through. On the plus side, the weather wizard on the radio said a fresh cold front was on its way from Alberta, bringing snow, straight-line winds, and probably a plague of mimes. I covered the eight miles to Allen

Park in just under an hour.

The Gamesman Inn wasn't any harder to find than the resting place of King Arthur; which in its glory days of stone-age lighting, smirking waiters, and pre-dawn regrets had been the whole point. It was tucked in a side street off Outer Drive between a sandy brick building with prosthetic limbs hanging in its display window and the kind of professional building whose tenants put "As seen on TV" in the Yellow Pages.

For all that, the place looked respectable enough, with an iron front and its name painted in pointy Gothic letters on a shield above an oak door with iron bands and probably a steel core. The intention was to suggest a London pub where Dickens and Thackeray would feel at home quaffing bitter ale over steak-and-kidney pie, and it was successful so far as impressionable Americans were concerned: just the sort of place George Hoyle would pick for his liaisons with Paula Lawes, whatever he'd said about subletting his faux-vintage-English house from someone else.

Parking was prohibited on the one-way street, but a small lot behind the building hosted a handful of cars at that early hour. I parked next to a Dumpster, got out, grasped the handle of a no-nonsense steel door with

CUSTOMERS WELCOME stenciled on it, and tugged. It didn't budge. I hadn't expected it to, but I had to try in spite of the hours posted on the door. I knocked, and went on knocking until a vest-pocket blonde in a handmaid's dust cap stuck her head outside. It came just to the top of my rib cage.

"I'm sorry, sir. We don't open for another hour."

"I'm not hungry." I showed my folder. The deputy's badge picked up the light from inside. "Is there anyone around who's been working here since the place changed hands?"

She gave my ID a pouty frown. Fog turned sluggishly in the partially enclosed area. I couldn't tell if she could read it.

"Are you the police?"

"Detective. No one's in trouble. I just want to ask some questions."

"Mr. Badderleigh is the man you want. Our manager. He was a bartender then, I think."

"Perfect."

Blue eyes the size of robin's eggs scanned me hair to heels. A suit and tie will get you places a T-shirt and jeans won't; it's a wonder the criminal class hasn't caught on. Anyway she opened the door the rest of the way and stood aside. She wore a starched white apron over a black velvet dress.

We followed a narrow corridor past a busy kitchen smelling thickly of frying onions, boiling cabbage, roasting meat, and lard — brunch fare a la Winston Churchill — into a square dim room where tin-shaded bulbs shed just enough light in the booths to see to eat. At that it would be like a hospital theater compared to the gin-some, sin-some paradise it had been in times past.

It was a genuine sports bar now, if the miniature Jumbo-Trons spotted around the room were any indication. They were dark now.

The little Dutch Maid signaled to me to stay put and approached a burly party supervising a table setup with his hands folded behind his back, Napoleon fashion. A head that was mostly untrained hair and eyebrows like soffits came up, turned my way, nodded. The hostess or whatever she was flounced off and after another moment spent scrutinizing the position of the flatware the burly party trundled my way, rocking on bowed legs and pigeon toes. He wore a green suede vest, brass buttons unfastened, a white dress shirt with cuffs the size of flowerpots, striped trousers, and shoes that matched the vest. The two halves of an old-fashioned do-it-yourself bow tie hung on either side of his open collar.

"Edgar Badderleigh." He caught my hand in one the size of a palm frond and let go. "I didn't get your rank, Mr. Walker." He had an accent you could cut with a cricket bat.

"I don't have one, Mr. Badderleigh. Badderleigh, is that Welsh?"

"Cornish. Penelope said you're a detective?"

"Private. I'm following up on an old police case. Penelope — her real name, or just something to go with the iron front?"

"It's the one she put on her résumé."

"Penelope said you worked here under the old management."

"Sad to say, yes. I was about to give my notice when the owner announced the sale. My ancestors belonged to the serving class, who took pride in waiting upon only those persons they respected."

"That wouldn't include a Recorders Court judge feeling up a legal secretary under the table."

"You said it. I didn't."

Crockery clacked. A vacuum choked on something solid. A cart rattled past carrying mops, brooms, and buckets, grazing my hip. "Is there a butler's pantry? I feel like a snag in the river."

"This way."

I trailed him, trying not to rock from side to side the way he did, like a career sailor on dry land. Childhood rickets, I thought, watching his trousers flap around calves not much bigger around than copper pipe. We turned into a short pine-paneled passage between doors marked BLOKES and BETTYS and through a plain unmarked door into a square room that was part office and part storage, with a desk made of black pebbled iron with a scratched Formica top and stacked cardboard cartons advertising brands of liquor and toilet paper. The walls were bare lath with old mortar squeezing out like lemon filling from between the slats. That made the building older than any dozen renovations. Fluorescent tubes mounted to the ceiling shed albino light, for once without a flicker.

There was no place to sit other than the chair behind the desk, a blown-out swivel patched with duct tape. Badderleigh, ever the gentleman, remained standing, with his hands behind his back. He lacked only a riding habit and a Russian wolfhound to complete the set.

"Whose idea was it?" I said. "Yours?"

"Idea?" The long stray hairs in his brow kept moving after he finished raising them.

I waved a hand, encompassing the building's whole interior. "The Dog-and-Whistle, yoiks and away, and so say all of us. A bit of the Old Blighty just spitting distance away from the Motor City. Or did that come first and the accent and Sherwood Forest family tree come after?"

Here was another poker face in my gallery. Even his tone was unrippled.

"You are a rum one, aren't you? Is this how you go about requesting my assistance in an official investigation, by insulting me?"

"I had to ask. It was the only way I could see to get past that stiff upper lip."

Something tugged at the corners of his wide mouth. It might have been a tic brought on by memories of Rorke's Drift. "I've been a citizen of this country twenty years, but I'll never get over how you Yanks think you've cornered the market on irony. No, the idea was the current owner's. He's a native of Los Angeles, which is where he spends all his time. I don't disregard the possibility that he took his inspiration from me. Incidentally, the stiff upper lip went out with the empire, or didn't you pay attention when the royal family was forced to issue a statement upon the occasion of Princess Diana's death?"

"No kidding, she died? A barkeep who can

pick out a Recorders Court judge from the general run of horndogs should remember a few other faces from the old days. What can you tell me about this one?"

That morning's *Free Press* had featured the Hoyle killing in Section A. Murders, especially those that took place in the suburbs, rarely drew that kind of attention, but when a retired ranking police officer was involved, the new bridge to Canada got kicked backed to Travel and Leisure. Someone had downloaded a head shot from the According to Hoyle web site. It was a good likeness, apart from the genial smile I'd never encountered on that horse face in person. I held out the clipping.

After a moment Badderleigh freed one of his hands from behind his back and took it. He frowned as far as his eyebrows, went around behind the desk, sat, and switched on a lamp mounted on a flexible tube. A pair of Delft-blue eyes that apparently didn't need correction scanned each line of text, then fixed on the image, about the size of a Christmas seal; stayed on it with all the concentration of a crime victim studying a mug shot. Finally he straightened and scaled the clipping across the desktop. "I'm sorry."

"Baloney."

"Sorry?"

"Poppycock. Balderdash. Whatever you Brits say when what you mean is bullshit. My pedigree doesn't stretch as far back as yours. I can't claim a Vidocq on my tree, but I've been a detective as long as you've slung drinks, and I know a positive ID when I see it in the making. The name may not ring Big Ben, but you know that face like your own."

The fingers attached to one of his flippers beat a tattoo on the desk. Factoring in the English temperament, he was frothing at the mouth.

"You must understand, we've been years overcoming a reputation —"

"Detroit isn't the West End," I said. "We've had bootleggers in the City-County Building who were issued those little gizmos that turn red lights green so the mayor didn't miss his three-martini lunch, and police chiefs who stashed their graft in the ceiling. The LCC won't yank your liquor license because you got involved in a homicide investigation. Especially when you cooperated.

"Give me a break, Badderleigh; that's not what's got your bowels in an uproar. Your man in Hollywood wouldn't be a front, would he? To spare you the embarrassment of a harder look at your interest in the Gamesman?"

The fingers stopped drumming. "I've never made a secret of my past mistakes. I lost a nice little family tavern in Cleveland Heights the third time a bartender I trusted — my ex-son-in-law, if you insist on details — sold spirits to underage customers. You can't maintain a business of this nature selling vegetable juice."

"You wouldn't be the first owner of a bar who let a virgin front for him," I said. "Hell, if you could patent the practice, our little metropolitan community would clear seven figures in royalties annually: We invented it the day Prohibition was repealed. That's where my plastic badge trumps the gold-plated bling they hand out at the academy. It's what puts the 'private' in 'private detective.' " That tasted like something past its sell-by date; I'd used it once too often on this deal. "What've I got to gain by selling you out? The cops might even stretch the point and pull my ticket as an accessory; enough of them don't like me to say I sat on the information since I took this job. This is the kind of place I'd take the family, if I had one. Who knows what'll move in once you're gone? Maybe something worse than what it was last time: An Internet café, maybe."

I stabbed Hoyle's long face with a forefinger, hoping that was enough. My throat was getting raspy from my summation to the jury.

He drew his eyebrows down to the corners of his mouth. Then he sat back and spread his hands. That was something no one had been able to get from his race since William the Conqueror.

TWENTY-EIGHT

"Is it too early for a drink?" he said.

"I've never understood that question."

Rising, he excused himself. He might even have made a slight bow, but that could have been just part of the overall impression. He was too British for Britain, just as some Texans are too Texas for Texas; get them off native territory and they spread out like knotweed. I killed time while he was gone opening a beige fire door and leaning out to admire a side street that paralleled the one in front of the building, two narrow lines running the opposite direction from the other. The fog was lifting, levitating all in one piece like a block of cream cheese. The sun of what promised to be a mild day poked out of its top; probably a tease.

I drew the door shut just as Badderleigh returned, lugging a brown enamel tray supporting a pitcher filled with scarlet liquid, two stout glasses, and a third thin one with green onions and celery stalks sticking up from it like pencils in a cup. He kicked the door shut with his heel and set the tray on the desk. I poured for us both, stirred mine, and laid aside the celery stick. A man could put his eye out if he wasn't careful.

He looked at his chair, hesitated. "I neglected to think this thing through."

I shook my head, slid a large carton up to the desk that was solid enough to support my one-eighty-five, and sat. That country-gentleman act was getting thick. I was beginning to think Great Uncle Nigel was more comfortable with a potato fork in his hand than a silver salver.

He could mix a cocktail, though. I couldn't tell where the tomato juice — fresh-squeezed and still smelling of the vine — left off and the Worchestershire sauce began. The gin was Bombay Sapphire, or some other label as distantly removed from fusel oil.

He tasted his drink, evaluated it, and dismissed the results all in a lump. So far as I could read those eyebrows his face was as legible as a good map, but they could be camouflage. His hands, wide as platters, were more honestly expressive. He flattened both on the desk, bracing for the worst.

"I never knew the man's name until this

moment," he said. "The people who tell a bartender all about their religious preferences and the state of their marriage rarely introduce themselves."

"No one would do both. I'd insist on anonymity myself if most people didn't pay by check. Apart from that our work's not so different."

"Yes. Well, men like Hoyle were bread-and-butter to the old Gamesman. He was one of our regulars. The same could not be said about the women who accompanied him. He changed them like shirts."

When I raised my glass to drink, the stiff photograph in my inside coat pocket rustled. It wasn't time to play that card. "He was a player."

"We used to call them libertines. Even 'whoremonger' dignifies them beyond their due. A prostitute sells her body to survive. A nymphomaniac is a slave to her infirmity. They're to be pitied, nothing worse. Animals like Hoyle — Is there a masculine counterpart for 'slut'?"

"It's your language. We just have it on loan. How often did he come around?"

"Often enough to call me Ed. You remember that song, 'Where Everybody Knows Your Name'? It applies only to bartenders. It almost never works the other direction."

"Always with a date?"

"Always. Well, except the last time."

"What time was that?"

The tomato juice had left a stain in his glass. He ran a finger inside the rim and sucked it dry. "It was a Tuesday, I know, because that was my day off, but the part-time man called in sick. I had tickets to the Fisher Theater that night; *Phantom.* I was still in a ruddy bad mood when he came in. I'm afraid I wasn't as polite to this fellow — Hoyle? — as a good counterman should be. That was unlike me, and so in spite of my feelings toward the man I was coming round the bar to apologize and offer him a drink on the house — the house being myself — when he nearly bally well bowled me over dashing for the exit."

"He stiffed you because you were rude?"

"No, he paid for his drink. I got the impression he was following someone and didn't want to be left behind."

It was time to play my hole card. I slid out Paula Lawes's photo and laid it on the desk. "They had a fight here one night."

He glanced, shook his head. "He was alone this particular evening. Come to think of it now, he might have stopped in specifically to make contact with the man he ran out after."

"Man?"

"One of our regulars. A police officer." He stopped turning the glass and looked up. "His name I know, because he was killed soon after. It was in the news for days."

Someone knocked. He said, "Yes?" and the small woman dressed like a barmaid came in carrying a big carton with a label from the Peninsula Paper Company.

"Ah, yes. The droll cocktail napkins." That acid undertone of contempt was purely Anglo-Saxon. "Over there, please."

In response to his gesture she placed the box on top of a stack. It seemed to be as light as a balloon.

"The Marcus Root case," I said when we were alone again. "I wish I'd been hired to crack that one. It keeps throwing itself in my face."

Badderleigh cocked a thumb toward the picture. "Who is this woman? I think I might have seen her in here."

I told him. "Oh, yes," he said. "She came in a number of times with Hoyle. I remember because he rarely escorted the same woman twice; and of course there was all that bit in the papers when she disappeared."

"The police must have asked you some

questions."

"Yes, but I couldn't tell them anything helpful. They showed me a picture of this man Hoyle, taken from his driving license, but they never told me his name. I said he'd been in with the Lawes woman. It didn't seem to excite them; but then the policemen are the same here as in England: wouldn't give you an 'Ouch' if you stabbed them in the bum."

"He'd already told them they were seeing each other. Did you report the other thing when they were here?"

"I never thought of it. It wasn't the night she vanished and when Root was killed. Are you suggesting Hoyle — ?"

"No, that's come out. But if Hoyle followed him the first time and didn't get what he wanted, he'd do it again and again, until he got something he wanted more." I sipped again and let the rest of the Bloody Mary in the glass. Now that I'd found a use for my wits I meant to keep them intact. "Thanks, Mr. Badderleigh, for the drink and information. Or do you prefer Ed?"

"My given name is Edgar. Given me, not you. Mr. Badderleigh, if you would be so kind."

TWENTY-NINE

Along with the opening bell of a typical workday, the traffic pattern in Allen Park had shifted, away from the northern incursion into Detroit toward homebodies running errands in town. Pickups and minivans puttered past the Gamesman's little parking lot, diehard cyclists in teardrop helmets and skintight Spandex pedaled hellfor-leather around the block, panting vapor under the fog, still climbing toward the sun with all the haste of a teenager crawling out of bed. But the signs pointed toward a break from winter; one of those Michigan particulars in which college coeds shed yesterday's parkas to sun themselves on the roof of Delta Sigma Phooey before the next blizzard hits. It's like Russia without the dogma; but it's what makes those six weeks of summer so bittersweet.

I kept the motor warming while waiting for a receptionist with a voice like chromed steel to put me through to Human Resources at GlobalCare Pharmaceuticals: That was the name I got from the recording when I called for Andrea Dawson's extension.

This one wasn't steely, but just as smooth, like sand sifted through a fine screen. The name was Van Fleet. He asked who was calling.

I'd given the receptionist my name, but it almost always slips through the seam between lines 1 and 2. I gave it again. "Ms. Andrea Dawson's cooperating in an investigation I'm conducting with the police in Detroit and Allen Park, a case involving an old acquaintance of hers. I'm finishing up the paperwork now. Can you tell me anything about her history with GlobalCare?"

"Without hesitation. She's one of our best."

I doodled in my pocket pad while he ticked off those parts of her employment record suitable for public consumption. She'd been with the place eight years, coming straight from a college course she'd signed up for after divorcing Mr. Dawson: "A lawyer, I understand; not an unpleasant parting, apparently. She refused a settlement. We thought that impressive; enough so that we agreed to let her work at home during her probationary period."

I stopped doodling. "Was that unusual?"

"More then than now. She explained that she performed better under those conditions, having taken all her courses online. Her duties were chiefly research, so the request wasn't difficult to fulfill. When after two years of flawless services we offered her a position with Information Services, she moved her operation to an office here."

"Information Services, that's Public Relations, isn't it?"

"It's more a matter of putting a human face on a commodity, like Betty Crocker or Snap, Crackle and Pop, only in her case she had the advantage of being real. And it's a nice face, both attractive and approachable. When she finally posted her picture on Facebook, our CEO directed me to interview her in person — to make sure there hadn't been any, um, enhancement in the posting. There wasn't, as it turned out. Thank goodness, because those of us who'd spoken with her on the phone were predisposed in her favor."

"The accent."

"Exactly. Who would doubt the word of a refined Southern belle?"

"So it was two years before she made face-to-face contact with anyone in your office?"

His chuckle was like flour pouring down ridged glass. "That sounds like a mystery woman; but I've been here fourteen years, and I can tell you I've never interviewed anyone who's more open and forthcoming."

"Isn't that the kiss-of-death for PR work?"

The chuckle choked off. "She's a spokesperson, not a spin artist."

"But she consulted with one: Paula Lawes."

"We have no record of that, but if she did, it would have been on her own responsibility, and at her own expense. The FDA might look unfavorably on such an association with our firm. If that's all, Mr. Walker — ?"

It wasn't, but it was as much as I would get out of the conversation. There'd been no hesitation between my dropping the Lawes bomb and his response. When it came to being open and forthcoming, Van Fleet was a human firewall.

I clicked off, hit Redial, and entered the extension number I'd memorized.

"Well, good morning, sugar," she said when I told her who was calling.

"You, too, Scarlett. How's every little thing at Chicamauga?"

"I'm not just sure which of us is more determined not to let Dixie rest in peace; we Southerners or you Yankees. You know, your accent's just as obvious to me as mine seems to be to you."

"Go on with you; it's as bland as custard pie. Are you free anytime today?"

"As air. Have you breathed it lately, by the way?" Keys rattled on her end. "I'm speaking at Wayne State at one. I should be able to give you ten minutes after the Q-and-A. It won't take that long. I've told you everything I knew."

"Maybe you can give me some tips on improving my image. It's taken some hits lately with the authorities."

"My consulting fee's forty an hour. Will your expense account stand it?"

"Provided I can deduct five dollars for every lie you tell me."

Air stirred. I couldn't tell if any of it had to do with breathing the local monoxide. "This much I can give you free of charge: Any negatives must be sandwiched between phrases of fulsome praise."

"I'm trying to please a client, not cover up a mass poisoning in India. Can I get in without a pass?"

"The centurion at the door should take her seat after the first thirty minutes. If not, you must serve your purgatory in the outside corridor." She gave me the number of the lecture room. I committed it to memory.

One more sample of Edgar Badderleigh's mixology would have had me searching for a pencil.

My belly drowned out the rumble of the 455 under the hood. The last time I took on fuel, George Hoyle was alive and counting his next take from Albert White. In Dearborn I steered into the curb in front of a restaurant with its English name lettered under a jumble of Arabic characters, where the lamb shank came to my table in a nest of new potatoes against a piped-in musical score composed by Suleiman the Magnificent on a diet of hashish, with a chaser of goat's milk and marinated dates. I was still tamping down the bleating when I pulled into the parking garage off the Cass Corridor.

Andrea Dawson's centurion turned out to be a young woman dressed in an unsuccessful attempt to conceal her physical charms behind a heavy sweater, hairpins, and clear-glass lenses in tortoiseshell frames. She explained that a ticket was required for attendance. I thanked her and took up a position in the paneled hallway, walking an unlit cigarette against the back of one hand: The ubiquitous red circle with a diagonal bar across it decorated the wall every eight feet. A hand-lettered placard on an easel advertised THE POWERS OF PERSUASION: AC-CENTUATING THE POSITIVE. The place smelled of chalk dust and patchouli, probably piped in since the introduction of white-erase board and airborne allergies.

A bell clanged: All out for Calculus, Phys. Ed., and Study Hall. The double doors swung wide, releasing a general rout of students of every age from acne to liver spots, regurgitating at warp speed the wisdom they'd just ingested.

I sidled in past them, swimming against the current.

I hadn't seen a picture of Andrea Dawson, but she was easy to spot, standing at the base of a horseshoe-shaped auditorium with stadium seating funneling down to a small stage where she stood leaning an elbow on a wooden lectern, speaking animatedly with a professor-type from the modern school: spiked hair, neck tattoo, torn jeans, and a gray sweatshirt with Einstein sticking out his tongue on the front. Her hair, worn in a shoulder-flip and teased to nosebleed height, was the color of polished copper and she wore a tailored mulberry-colored jacket on top of a black turtleneck, her flared lapels spread in a heart shape, framing a pair of breasts under which nothing could grow in the shade. Notwithstanding that, her hips curved out and then in, wineglass fashion, under a gray hobble skirt. Runners' calves in black leggings and long narrow feet strapped into open-toed shoes to match the jacket. Her face was pleasingly plump, rouged artistically, with wide-set eyes, a long upper lip with a deep dimple, and a nose not quite too small to spoil the effect. She could have used more chin, but the lips, carved by the dimple, would have put the final touches on a Tintoretto.

Small wonder Van Fleet had promoted her on the spot. A face and a body like that, complete with the magnolia brush to her speech, could make a bottle of E. coli taste like almond M&M's.

I was still doing acrobatics with the unlit cigarette. I tucked it back into the pack and the pack back into my inside pocket and waited at the top of the tier of seats while Dr. Grunge took a slim white hand, managed not to kiss it on the return, and floated up the steps grinning in his five-o'clock shadow. I waited until he was outside, then stepped over and flipped up the hinged doorstop gizmo with a toe. The heavy door whooshed shut against the pressure of the pneumatic closer.

Andrea Dawson stepped back behind the lectern to shuffle her notes and slide them into an eggplant-colored leather briefcase with twin handles.

"Congratulations," I said. "Looks like you hit it into the cheap seats."

The place had fine acoustics. I'd barely spoken above a murmur, but every syllable seemed to have reached the woman on the stage. She looked up with a smile quivering on the edge of caution. "Thank you, sugar. Yes, it seemed to go over quite well. Are you with the university?"

"Amos Walker. We spoke over the phone."

"Oh." She was accustomed to fielding questions and accusations without moving a muscle in her face. "I thought we'd covered everything about poor Paula."

"She's not so poor. If she can prove how much her husband knew about the engagement ring he gave her, she'll never have to spend another day spinning silk out of burlap."

The smile went away. The expression now was attentive and not at all cautious in appearance. "You-all have your tenses mixed up, I'm afraid. And it isn't polite to speak ill of the dead."

"Wrong note," I said. "A real clinker. No Southerner says 'you-all' unless she's addressing more than one person. As long as you were going to all the trouble to change your looks and your history, you should have taken time to hire a voice coach. George Hoyle was a stickler when it came to accents — he went ballistic just because one of his readers slipped from Southampton to West Hollywood — but if you went to him for help, it didn't take as well as it should have."

"I never met the man. Is it a crime to sweeten one's speech in pursuit of a good job? If you were to start prosecuting folks for fudging their résumés —"

"Sure you met him. I doubt even an expert face job would fool someone who worked for the Gamesman as long as my source did, especially when it belongs to the only woman who ever came there with Hoyle more than once.

"I didn't mix up my tenses. You did. Over the phone you said, 'Paula's an only child.' Is, not was. No one would speak of someone in the present tense after as many years as she'd been considered dead. John Alderdyce tagged Lawes for your murder when he made the same slip, only in reverse. I was too preoccupied with all the twists the case was taking to jump on it. I forgot to remember; a serious flaw in a detective. But it kept festering, like a splinter in my foot. It might still be, if not for my insomnia. I woke up last midnight, positive Paula Lawes is alive."

The silver bells in her throat tinkled. "That's your evidence? A slip of the tongue and a restless night?"

"Proof is the cops' job. I'm just making small talk."

I was moving, descending the long flight of broad steps leading between rows of seats down to the stage, feeling my way with my feet. One of her hands remained inside the briefcase she was holding and I didn't want to take my eyes off it. The university was a gun-free zone, by law; I'd left the Ruger behind in the car. Talking was the only weapon I had.

"If Paula fought with Hoyle, it was because she made him jealous, being friendly with Marcus Root that night in the Gamesman. Of course, the only reason to accept the fact that there *was* a fight was what you told me about that night Paula was supposed to have shown up at your house looking for a sympathetic ear. Whether it happened or not, Hoyle was charged up enough to come back to the bar, which was a hangout for Root and his fellow officers, and follow him when he left, to see if he linked up with Paula. Thing about these tomcats is they can't stand any woman treating them the way they do women in general."

"That much is true. When a woman behaves that way, they say she's a bitch in heat."

"You'll be glad to know at least one man shares your opinion. He thought 'whoremonger' was still too genteel for the Hoyles of this world."

"I think you'd better stop where you are, Mr. Walker. You know how things are in universities these days. If I were to scream —" The hand inside the briefcase moved.

I stopped three steps from the bottom, arms hanging at my sides. I turned my head from side to side, studying her face at close range. "Women have the advantage in one thing. Changing hairstyle and color go a long way toward altering their looks. You put on a few pounds, but on a Daughter of the Confederacy they look good. The rest was modern medicine.

"You got your money's worth and more," I went on. "I doubt even Lawes would recognize you after all this time. The bone structure's the same, eyes the same color. Breaking the cheek straps and the bridge of the nose to reset them would slow down the recovery by months, and if you wore contacts there was always the chance of losing one and someone noticing, which leads to thinking. No, I think you took it as far as it could go."

With the smile dead as dust she resembled her photos, or at least someone who was related by blood to the woman who'd posed for them. Despite the corn-fed curves she had the lean, almost feral look of a horse-woman; someone athletic, anyway. I wouldn't lay a bet as to whether my reflexes would be any match for hers.

"And *I* think," she said, "that you're taking the long way around the barn when you should come out and say what you mean."

I grinned. That allowed me to take in extra oxygen between my teeth. I needed all I could get. "The dialogue's spot on, but you forgot the accent. Without the magnolias, it's pure Rust Belt. Welcome back, Paula. A lot of people have been asking for you."

THIRTY

The briefcase took a jump, along with my heart; but it was just her body reacting to the shock. I shifted my weight to my good leg anyway. I could have used another step closer. I'd made longer tackles, but back then I'd had youth on my side. What I still had was words.

"I'm not just spinning yarns from spring fog. Whatever plastic surgeon made Andrea Dawson out of Paula Lawes would keep records, even if he thought there was something smelly about the reasons you gave. A nose job's one thing, eye work's another, but a drastic makeover raises questions. He'd keep at least a private file, in case it came back on him by way of the medical board or the police.

"Where'd you go, Mexico?" I shook my head. "Canada makes better sense. It's only minutes away from where your car was found abandoned. The chances of being identified were a lot less than if you made the trip through six states. More convenient for you, but also for the FBI. Our neighbors to the north are cooperative, and their files are in better order."

There was a sea change in her expression. If I let my imagination run free, I'd have seen several thousand dollars' worth of medical reconstruction melt away, leaving Paula Lawes standing behind that lectern, unchanged after six years. For sure Andrea Dawson's honeyed tones were history. The hand hidden inside the briefcase stopped stirring; she straightened, looking me square in both eyes with Paula Lawes's.

"What of it?" she said. "Where's the crime in trading a life that had become unbearable for another? There were times when I actually envied battered wives; they at least have shelters to go to, and a support group as big as the majority of the population. A woman trapped in an arid marriage is a joke, and hardly an object of pity. If I come off as overly poetic, it's because I've had years to work on the speech.

"What's the worst that can happen? Divorce? I never knew a divorcée who didn't drag around all the same baggage into so-called independence. It's common knowledge: That's why GlobalCare was so quick to accept the lawyer ex-husband I made up to explain my long absence from the workforce. I had money; still have. Don't think I did all this on a whim, without taking steps to secure it. As long as account numbers and signatures check out, foreign banks couldn't care less about a client's status; although there are certain complications to be overcome when she's been declared dead. There was a time factor involved."

I worked my thigh muscles, to keep them from locking. As long as that hand was out of sight I was an obstacle. A trapped animal is the most dangerous.

"You haven't committed a real crime — yet. Rigging your own disappearance made for an expensive investigation, but after all this time I doubt anyone would bother to collect. A woman who wore a ring that's supposed to be a symbol of commitment, but that turns out to be a chunk of hot ice, has unresolved issues. Black-mailing her ex would be one way of obtaining a resolution, if only to make him sweat; the money paid for your silence might be nothing more than a number on the scoreboard, proof you'd won. Just what did you get out of Marcus Root?"

"I was no starry-eyed wife. I had doubts about that ring from the start; call it woman's intuition, but I saw something in Francis' eyes when he slipped it on my finger. It festered; your word, and appropriate. A woman can live with a thing for years, piling grievance upon grievance, until it becomes a symbol of something more important.

"I helped elect a governor," she said. "That gave me a passport into places a civilian can't enter. Marcus had a reputation for dealing with the local gangs; just what it was, its nature, didn't concern me. When I found out about the robbery in Southfield, and saw the inventory of what was stolen, I went to him with what I had. He wanted to run for president of the Detroit Police Officers Association, which represents most of the officers in the metropolitan area. Possibly it was his way of breaking off his arrangement with his commander, but that didn't concern me. In return for my assistance in his campaign, he gave me this."

The hand came out of the briefcase; I braced myself for the tackle.

The hand came out holding a slim spiral notepad.

I relaxed my muscles. Circulation tingled all the way up my thigh. "A lot of people have been looking for that. The cops think it was taken from Root's patrol car after he was murdered, to cover up what he wrote about the scene of your disappearance."

"There's nothing in it about that; he gave it to me before that night. It does contain everything he found out about the jewelry theft and how much Francis knew about the circumstances when he bought the ring from one of the robbers. You're welcome to it, for what it's worth. He only gave it to me to prove he'd made a good-faith effort."

She held it out: just like that. I came down the last three steps and took it.

"It's what you wanted, isn't it? Like everything else someone wants so badly, it's disappointing." She finished shoveling paperwork into the case and snapped it shut. "We're finished here, Mr. Walker. If you don't mind — or even if you do — I'm expected back at GlobalCare. A men's sexual enhancement drug we've been selling is facing a class-action lawsuit: something about kidney disease. I'm needed to spin it into a minor infection."

I held up both hands, one gripping the notebook. I hadn't been hired to play watchdog over Big Pharm.

"We're almost done," I said.

She paused with both hands on the briefcase. "What more could there be?"

"Not much; only everything. I had all

these answers before I came; I only needed to hear them for the record. The only question I couldn't answer myself is why you broke into my house and left the ring. If what you say about the notebook is true, the ring was your only hole card. Why give it up?"

Her face went blank, almost stupid. It was Paula Lawes's now; there was no trace of Andrea Dawson's apart from the superficial.

"How could I have done that?" she said. "I didn't know you existed until you called me the other day."

I nodded. I didn't know why I hadn't come up with it before. I was as stupid as she looked, only without her excuse.

We spoke a bit more. I had all I needed then. I stepped back and watched her slide her briefcase under her arm and climb the stairs to the exit.

THIRTY-ONE

The day was fine, according to the standards of April on the Great Lakes. The sun was as bright as a new coin, and some birds were cautiously trying out their throats, with due regard to a possible wind shift from Ontario. The rip and snarl of chainsaws — as much a part of the vernal equinox as grumpy crickets and thawing frogs — rang throughout the city of Redford. Tree limbs, waterlogged by a week of relentless weeping rain, had cracked through at the groin and transformed each block into an obstacle course of budding branches and shattered mailboxes. John Alderdyce stood in his front yard in a striped shirt with the sleeves rolled to his elbows and his hands in the pockets of pressed black jeans, watching a hardhat crew turning a stately maple into kindling.

I pulled the Cutlass into the nearest safe curb, got out, and shouted at his back: "I'm surprised you're not up there buzzing away with the hired help."

"Marilee's orders," he said, turning without a sign I'd startled him. "Thirty years facing down punks hopped up to the eyebrows and armed to the teeth, and she's afraid I'll cut my arm off doing yard work."

I jerked my head and we walked down the sidewalk away from the racket. "How's it going with Albanian Al?"

"Zip. Tried bluffing his way into a ticket-of-leave. Kindergarten stuff, fell apart in the details. This new breed isn't a patch on the old; it's enough to make you miss the good old days of Young Boys, Incorporated. He wasn't there when the merch was sold. He can't connect Lawes to the hot ring, let alone swear he knew about the watchman who got squiffed during the heist and make it convincing enough to stand up under an amateur cross in court. I wasted my career on shit like that. Now it turns out I'm wasting my retirement."

"Too bad." I unwrapped the ring from its twist of tissue and held it out.

He stopped walking, but didn't take his hands from his pockets. "Anything?"

"Nothing; not even the murder you wanted to lay on Lawes first." I told him what I had, beginning with Badderleigh and finishing with Andrea Dawson/Paula Lawes.

"The groundwork started early," I said. "While Andrea's bosses at the drug company thought she was working at home, she called her own line at Baylor and Baylor regularly, establishing a business relationship with Paula. It helped create the illusion of two women co-existing, long before Paula's vanishing act."

We were still stopped on the sidewalk. He took the ring, turned it over in his fingers, pocketed it. "So you literally dreamed that up, and ran with it anyway."

"It fit the facts."

"Any theory will if you cook it. We need prints, DNA —"

"You won't get them. There's no crime in taking it on the ankles when no one's chasing you. Anyone can get a face job and change her name."

"She'd need a Social Security number to match."

"You know the anthem better than I do," I said. "The real Andrea Dawson died in infancy forty years ago, probably in some Southern state. If the law really wanted identity thieves to give up robbing graves, it'd start cross-referencing birth and death records. The feds in Paula's situation might make a case based on false representation, but what's that to you? Her husband's the

283

one you want."

"If Paula didn't put the ring in your house, who did?"

"That's why I'm going where I'm going next. There's only one person in this mess who doesn't care whether she's alive or dead."

He waited. That face would stand up to any number of shipwrecks, brush away the shattered masts and bowsprits, and come out looking no more the worse for wear. "I'm guessing you'll run to me with what you find out. And Deb Stonesmith," he added; retirement still stuck in his craw.

"Stonesmith wants the story before it breaks. That's a favor I owe her. Paula's not a police case now, unless I decide to press charges for breaking-and-entering."

"You never have before. Why start now?"

"You'll turn in the ring, of course. It belongs to the company that insured the shop. You may want to have this for a souvenir." I took a dilapidated notepad from another pocket and held it up. The creased cardboard cover hung crookedly where it had torn loose of the metal spiral.

This he took without pausing. "If this is what I think it is, a lot of people have been looking for it."

"That's what I said when Andrea — let's

call her Paula — gave it to me. I read it. You won't find anything interesting. Root couldn't find anything more about the circumstances of how that ring came into private possession than you could. There's nothing on Paula's disappearance, of course; it hadn't happened yet. It bears out her claim that he gave it to her and that it wasn't stolen from his corpse. Maybe he thought she could bluff Lawes with it. He wanted to run for president of the police union, she said, and he wanted her help as a kingmaker. Call me sentimental, but I like to think he wanted to make up for past mistakes by helping out his brothers in blue."

"You're sentimental. I'm for disinterring him and bringing him up on charges. You really think Paula wanted to blackmail Lawes?"

"Not that it matters — Root can't testify, and she'd be a fool to confess — but it's the only reason she'd go to the trouble to find out how the ring got into Lawes's hands. Even if he didn't have the liquid assets necessary to satisfy her, that million-dollar policy he took out on both their lives would cash out to a tidy piece of change."

We'd stopped at the end of the block and were facing each other. He made a gesture toward my breast pocket I remembered from times past. I dealt him a cigarette from the pack and lit it. "I wish you'd make up your mind," I said.

"I gave up drinking two years ago. A man needs to have something he can quit." He blew twin jets out his nose. "Shit. I don't think I can get used to not wanting to nail Lawes for his wife. Even if I could make a case for receiving stolen property — with or without complicity in robbery homicide — it'd be like filling up on junk food; bloated, not satisfied. What am I supposed to fill my time with now?"

We turned around and started back toward his house. "There's always Bingo."

"You know, you're not so sunny yourself. You should be doing handsprings. Unless you're holding back — which if you're not would have no precedent — this is one job where you weren't shot at, beaten up, or arrested."

"You're forgetting another concussion for my collection."

"You've built up so much scar tissue one more won't matter. As far as cases go, this time you're barely used."

"The case isn't finished yet."

"Get the hell off my lawn." He went back to watch the destruction.

A couple of sharpies in peaked lapels and jewel-colored shirt-and-necktie sets loitered in front of the Coleman A. Young Municipal Center, diddling tablets the size of subway tiles. They were either toppling foreign governments or playing football with the cast of *The Avengers.* I walked in past them and rode the elevator alone to Fifteen.

The strawberry blonde in Reception recognized me through her eyeglasses. She buzzed Lawes's office and said he'd be with me in a few minutes. Just then Holly Pride came in: everything the same as in dress rehearsal, a few days and a thousand years ago. She was back in vertigo mode, only it seemed to me her bangs angled back the other way, her hip-hugging red skirt cut on the opposite bias with a bolero jacket tugged down over the belt, red on one side of the buttons, gray on the other.

"Oh, Mr. Walker."

"Don't bother," I said. "I know you've got a monitor or something in your office. Nobody's timing is that good twice in a row."

"As disagreeable as ever, I see. Have you come with news about Paula?"

"Yeah, but this time I'll talk to you first."

Once again she opened the door to her office and held it while I went in and looked at the river, a deep Windex blue. The fog had burned off; all the scene needed was a scattering of bright-colored sails to pose for a picture postcard in the airport, but it was still too early for that. Any day now the lid would slam back down and the parkas and galoshes come back out.

For the second time she leaned back against the plain desk, crossed her ankles and her arms, and blinded me with the diamond on her left hand.

I pointed at it. "It's got a good half-carat on the one he gave Paula. He show you the bill of sale?"

"He told you that wasn't the ring he gave her."

"No, he said he couldn't remember. I half believe him, even now. I imagine after what happened under some previous administrations he deals his city contracts under a strong microscope. He's gotten so used to operating on the up-and-up he might be forgiven blocking out mistakes of the past. If we accept that, it's likely he didn't know the ring had blood on it. Why should he? What thief would volunteer the information and open himself up to a murder charge?"

"I have no idea what you're talking about."

"You ladies need new material," I said. "That's just what Paula said."

She uncrossed her limbs and straightened. The rouge on her cheeks, expertly applied as it was, stood out like reflectors against the sudden pallor. "You found her?"

"Now I'm insulted. It's what Lawes hired me to do, dead or alive, and since you knew she was alive you should have had enough faith in my ability to track her down."

"How would I know —"

Her intercom buzzed, sparing me the burden of composing another caustic comment.

She reached over and flipped the switch. The receptionist's voice crackled through the speaker. "Mr. Lawes is ready to see Mr. Walker."

"In a minute, Gretchen." She turned it off and assumed her earlier position. That short diversion had given her the chance to change strategies. Some people are like that.

"I won't insult us both," she said. "You've been working. You're right. In our responsibility to the city, we analyze the business practices of the contractors who bid on public works; that includes the health benefits they offer their employees. Francis can't do everything, so that part falls to me.

I met Andrea Dawson while investigating GlobalCare Pharmaceuticals.

"I didn't recognize her at first. You've seen her. The surgeon she selected must love Canada, because he could write his own ticket in Hollywood. But I knew Paula when I was just the receptionist here, early in her marriage to Francis. You know how you sometimes meet someone, and certain characteristics — little gestures, the way they hold their head, and of course the register of their voice — despite the distraction of a broad accent — remind you of someone you used to know?" She didn't wait for an answer. "Well, it doesn't happen frequently, but often enough that you chalk it up to certain types of personality, like automobiles belonging to the same line. But when those similarities are so strong they become distracting, you start to speculate. You argue with yourself — no, so-and-so would be too old now, or should recognize you as well, is dead. It doesn't take, though. The sensation is so strong it trumps all the facts on the other side."

"Who cracked first?" I said.

"She did, over a business lunch in the London Chop House; as public a place as that, can you imagine? But the din of the place, the dishes being served, the racket coming from the kitchen, the customers' conversation, is better than the privacy of a closed room.

"She got sick of her dry-hump of a marriage; I won't wear out your patience with the details. They're always dreary, aren't they?"

"Not always, but the ones that aren't are just plain scary. What about the ring?"

"That came much later, in the quiet of her office. She suspected it was stolen the day he gave it to her; something about his attitude, and the fact that there was no box. She didn't say anything then. It was a good match for her, and like most people in that situation — men *and* women — she didn't ask the questions she didn't want to know the answers to. But she'd learned just enough from her police friend to make her nervous about keeping it around. It was nothing anyone could take to court, but —"

"I know. I read Marcus Root's notebook."

"Where better else to hide it from Francis than with his fiancée? You see, I'm smarter than she was when they were engaged — more experienced, anyway. I know just enough about him that the information was no surprise."

"But not so much you'd break off the engagement."

Her smile was as crooked as her bangs and the hem of her skirt. "You don't know my background, Mr. Walker. I came from nothing, with no prospects. If you think answering the phone and taking messages carries a promise of advancement, you haven't read many success stories.

"I felt I owed Paula the favor of safeguarding that ring. If she hadn't left him, I'd never have had the chance to take her place. That alone promoted me to second-in-command. And having the ring gave me an ace in the hole in case he changed his mind about marrying me, with all the benefits that carries."

"Then why give it up? Good housebreaking, by the way. Especially for an amateur."

"Who said I was an amateur? I told you I came from nothing. One learns to get along." She rolled her shoulders. "I did some research based on what Root gave Paula. When I found out someone had been killed in order to get that ring to Francis, I got scared. Theft is one thing; murder's the gift that keeps on giving. That's why I tried to hire you away before you found out Paula was alive, to stop that train. When you wouldn't cooperate, I transferred possession of the evidence to you. That way, when things blew up, Francis wouldn't blame it

292

on me. I've always known he was unscrupulous, but finding out just what he's capable of —"

"And just what is that?"

The hinges on the door were well-oiled. My back was to it, and I was blocking Holly's view. We didn't know Lawes was here until he spoke. If the element of surprise didn't make him the center of attention, the gun in his hand did.

THIRTY-TWO

I'd seen it once before, lying on the carpet next to Lawes's bed. Even with its extended barrel, the Glock was smaller than Py's huge magnum, but it looked bigger in Lawes's life-size fist. It was big enough in any case: I hadn't thought to strap my Ruger back on after leaving Wayne State University. Someday, just for kicks, I'll sit down, tot up all the mistakes I've made against the smart moves, and pay due respect to the miracle of dumb luck.

The pistol looked longer yet with the addition of an attachment threaded to the end of the barrel, sausage-shaped with a brushed-steel finish: a noise suppressor. That turned my knees to water.

I raised my hands without waiting for direction.

He'd been drinking. His suit, dove gray with a silvery sheen, was pressed and his blue silk tie was snugged to the notch of his shirt collar. His abundance of fair hair was brushed back neatly. But his eyes were unfocused and his mouth slack; not unfocused enough, or slack enough. A firearm employed in the closeness of a room doesn't need precision.

"Graft job, this," I said, "like all government buildings. You can hear a flea sneeze in a box of cotton on the other side of the door."

"I heard enough. So Paula's still among the living. That's one rap they can't hang me with."

"You're welcome. You don't have to pay me now. I'll send you a bill with my report."

"Forget the report. I was listening, remember? Just give me the notebook and the ring." He held out his free hand.

"You should've waited to hear the rest. The police have them."

He jacked his jaw up into position, gestured at Holly with the pistol. "Search him. Make it convincing."

"Fran—"

He'd been pointing the gun at the middle ground between us. Now he swung it directly on her.

She turned back toward me. Her hands shook, but they found my wallet, keys, notepad, and pencil. She examined all these and returned them to their pockets, shook her head at Lawes.

"Not even a weapon," he said, pointing his at me. "I've been reading too much sensational fiction. I thought all you hard-boiled dicks went heeled."

"Sorry. I'm a three-minute egg."

He looked at Holly. "I sent Gretchen to lunch. She works too hard. You know, I think she has her eyes on your job. You set a dangerous precedent."

"I guess you're kicking me to the curb." Her voice wobbled a little. I gave her credit for finding it at all.

I said, "You're overreacting, Lawes. Even if the cops manage to make a case, it won't go any further than receiving stolen property. There's nothing to tie you to murder. You'd get off with probation, maybe even keep your job. The city's kept worse on the payroll."

"I wish you were as dumb as you pretend, Walker. I'm serious. Then I wouldn't have to trouble my friends with disposing of two bodies from the eleventh floor of a high-traffic building."

Holly might have taken in her breath; but that might as well have been me. I nodded. "I can guess who your friends are. The cops know all their hangouts. The raid on Monte

Carlo's was to the garden-variety crash-and-grab what robbing the Louvre is to a mugging on Hastings. It was a distribution center for retailers across the country, so the stakes were high. Your friends bought the truck for cash, to minimize the chances of being picked up on the way to or from the heist. They had the equipment to tear out the vault where the most valuable stuff was kept, and someone who knew how to blow it once they were out of earshot. That takes financing.

"It was your job from the start," I went on. "No city employee could manage that on his pay. My guess is you were smarter than the crooks you replaced, spreading the jobs evenly, taking smaller kickbacks from more contractors, and staying under the radar."

"You're smart too." His smile was tight; no slack now. He was growing more sober by the second.

I talked some more; he might think it rude to shoot someone in the middle of a sentence. "Any killing that occurs in the course of a robbery is related directly to everyone involved. It makes you an accessory both before and after the fact. That ring can still wind up around your neck, Lawes, no matter what happens to us. John Alderdyce has worked up too much of a mad against you to let go. Eliminating us isn't worth it."

That had the effect I wanted. His face went stupid. Then his eyes turned bleak. "I've gone too far now to go back, though, haven't I?"

That was the effect I'd hoped would miss him.

"Disposing of you shouldn't be too difficult," he said to me. "Your work, I'm sure you've made your share of enemies on both sides of the law. When you turn up on a trash heap, I don't suppose the taxpayers will take a big hit on the investigation. Holly — well, I'll figure something out. Two unexplained disappearances in one man's domestic life may be asking a lot for the authorities to swallow, but if I work it right, you won't be in a position to cause the kind of inconvenience Paula did; and since we never consummated the engagement, I won't have to go through the messy business of proving you dead." Suddenly his face softened. "I did want to marry you, put the past far enough behind it wouldn't catch up. There'd be time to start over somewhere, with a stake to support us."

While he was talking to her I cast my glance around for something to throw. I'd have to lunge for the telephone-intercom set on the desk, and there were the wires to hang me up; Lawes wasn't so drunk his reflexes wouldn't prove more than a match, and the pistol would do the rest. The pictures on the walls might as well have been hanging in the British Museum for all the access I had to them.

No, there was only one thing handy.

It was ungentlemanly as hell. I grabbed hold of Holly with both hands, squeezing her arms hard enough to leave bruises, and hurled her at the man holding the gun; hurled her as if I were George Washington heaving all the gold in the U.S. Treasury across the Potomac.

THIRTY-THREE

Somewhere in the stygian tunnels of Detroit Receiving Hospital, the *Golden Girls* were bickering over a communal cheesecake. Somewhere in the world they're doing the same thing, every minute of every day. A TV sitcom that's run its course is the nearest thing we have to a perpetual motion machine.

I sat in a generic waiting room browsing among the unfamiliar faces in a two-month-old issue of *People,* wanting a smoke but knowing that some overweight health-care professional in a flowered smock would come looking for me the minute I left.

I had the place to myself. All the heavy traffic was outside Emergency, where they stacked the GSWs, DUIs, and DOAs before dispatching them to their destinations. The staff at Receiving specializes in removing slugs, drawing blood, and hanging tags on toes. I'd spent time there in the past, on gurneys and on hard benches. A stale magazine filled with glamorous strangers and regular doses of canned laughter were a distinct improvement.

"Man, I hope for his sake the guy that decorated one of these places the first time took out a patent. He'd be laying on a beach somewhere next to the inventor of the orange construction barrel."

I looked up at John Alderdyce coming in from the hall. He wore a made-to-order outfit fashioned from raw silk and starched linen. I said, "I thought all you retirees turned your business wear into grease rags."

"Save that for some pensioner. I've got a job." He sat on the settee opposite mine and showed me a gold-and-enamel shield pinned to a stiff leather folder. "Special Consultant to the Detective Division, as of this morning."

"I didn't know the department had one."

"Neither did the department, until it tagged me. My first job's to sweat Albanian Al Zog, our friendly incarcerated gangbanger, in partnership with Oakes Steadman, on loan from the state police. We already know he planned to squeeze Francis X. Lawes for bankrolling the Monte Carlo job once his parole comes up in three years and change; all we need is for Al to confirm it. Which he will, if he doesn't want to do his full bit for failing to cooperate in a homicide investigation."

"You're welcome."

"Did Lieutenant Stonesmith say thanks?"

"She didn't have to. She'd already paid for it. What about that clumsy bluff Zog tried to run about Lawes buying the hot ring, the one with all the holes in it?"

"He's smarter than he looks, using a transparently phony confession as a stone-walling tactic. It was good enough to fool some pretty sharp interrogators in Robbery Armed."

"Albanians are clever. We didn't even know the country was there until they raised the Iron Curtain."

"Speaking of Steadman," he said, "he and Kid Kong found George Hoyle's nest-egg hidden in his house: A smartphone with a picture of the low-rider Albert White borrowed from the impound, plate and all, time- and date-stamped. Nothing on that Impala Marcus Root was following; probably just a random distraction. Oh, and a sign in the background advertising the Lions' training camp. That puts the car a couple of blocks from where Root was killed."

"Nice to know the team's good for something. Do you think Hoyle saw the whole deal?"

"We'll never know, without his testimony; but who needs it? White's facing a court where there's no appeal."

"I didn't know you were so devout."

He lifted his brows, jerking his thumb back over his shoulder.

I flipped the magazine shut and scaled it at the nearest table. "She's getting dressed, waiting for her release to come through by tramp steamer. I'm her ride."

"Damned decent of you, considering you're the reason she's here."

"She was light enough to throw and heavy enough for the job. Where's Lawes in the system?"

"Booked and printed, hollering lawyer. Prosecutor's pushing for no bail. He'll settle for Lawes's passport and an electronic tether. He's subpoenaing Paula, by the way."

"You're welcome for that too. For what it's worth. She doesn't have anything concrete."

"He'll call her as a reverse character witness. Judge'll throw it out, but it'll take more than that to dig the worm out of the minds of the jury." He rearranged his big shoulders; somewhere on the other side of the earth a tidal wave wiped out a village.

"We'll be lucky to get him five years in minimum security on the felony homicide; maybe two more for the attempt on you and Pride. If we can get the feds involved, some of the contractors he got to pay for play may get nervous and turn state's evidence; that's a game-changer. These days, public corruption draws more fire than the murder of a bookkeeper."

A nurse came in, as pretty and cheerful as a party balloon. "Mr. Walker? She's all yours."

I stood. To Alderdyce: "What's Marilee think of your new job?"

"Why don't you ask her?"

"I'd rather face another gun."

We shook hands.

Holly Pride was sitting in a wheelchair when I entered her room, clutching a plastic bag containing her personal stuff on her lap. She had on the same outfit she'd worn when I brought her to the hospital after turning Lawes over to the police. Her crazy crooked bangs were in order and her outfit didn't show many wrinkles. That was what would have taken most of the time while I waited. The cast on her right ankle glared antiseptic white where her foot was propped on the flat metal doohickey that swung out from in front of the wheels.

"Should I sign it?" I said.

"Artists usually sign their work. Did you have to use me as a weapon?" She rubbed her upper arms; it was anyone's bet which healed first, the fractured ankle or the bruises my fingers had left.

"I don't think so well on my feet. Anyway, he let go of the gun. I haven't made a circus catch like that since the army." I worked the fingers of my right hand. I'd backhanded the Glock across Lawes's mouth, scraping my knuckles on his teeth. "If it means anything, I think he did love you enough to marry."

"It doesn't. I was a means to an end, like all his other shortcuts." She stopped rubbing her arms. "I'll have to testify, won't I?"

"Not soon. Lawes's lawyer will get the trial date put off as long as he can while the noise dies down in the press. You'll be on your feet making the rounds of the employment agencies before you're summoned."

"I won't mind. I was looking for a job when I met Fran. You wouldn't need an experienced receptionist, by any chance?"

"There's not enough to receive. I spend most of my working day trying to avoid getting caught in the World Wide Web."

She smiled. "Well, maybe we can figure

something out together. Meanwhile you can take me to lunch; someplace without a dress code." She smoothed her skirt. "I've already passed twice on the low-sodium, no-sugar-added, overcooked hogslop they dish up here."

"I know a joint where the food is twice as tasteless and almost as cold." I stepped behind the chair and grasped the handles. "Spot me a few bucks? I'm having trouble lately collecting from clients."

ABOUT THE AUTHOR

Loren D. Estleman is author of more than seventy novels. Winner of four Shamus Awards, five Spur Awards, and three Western Heritage Awards, he lives in Michigan with his wife, author Deborah Morgan. www.lorenestleman.com

The employees of Thorndike Press hope you have enjoyed this Large Print book. All our Thorndike, Wheeler, and Kennebec Large Print titles are designed for easy reading, and all our books are made to last. Other Thorndike Press Large Print books are available at your library, through selected bookstores, or directly from us.

For information about titles, please call:
(800) 223-1244

or visit our website at:
gale.com/thorndike

To share your comments, please write:

Publisher
Thorndike Press
10 Water St., Suite 310
Waterville, ME 04901